Believe in Forever

Amy Sparling

Dedication

This book is for my Instagram followers. Your enthusiasm and excitement for Jett's series has made it so much more fun to write! Thank you all for being so supportive. <3

Chapter 1

KeaNNa

Going back to school after Thanksgiving holiday is like marching into jail on Monday morning. We'd had the whole week off school and it was glorious. I spent every moment with Jett or my new parents or both, and I'd finally met my new grandparents. Becca's dad is the Lawson Police Chief and her mom is really sweet—almost as sweet as Becca. I haven't met Park's parents yet but they're supposed to come down for Christmas. Park said that in the summer he'll take us to California to hang out with them at their beach house and I couldn't be more excited. By then, my baby brother or sister will be here so it'll be even more of an adventure.

Jett and D'andre are having a friendly guy argument about which professional supercross racer is going to win the championship, so I eat my blueberry muffin in silence, preferring to watch the two of them go at it. I still don't know enough about professional supercross to comment. I do know that those guys are all pretty attractive and the girls who hang out at The Track fawn over them constantly. The most popular guys have social media profiles filled with self-taken sexy photos of themselves, usually shirtless and standing near a dirt bike.

My mind wanders off while Jett begins what I'm sure is a well-thought out argument for his favorite racer. I think about Jett's social media profiles and how he hardly ever used them before we met. (I know, because I stalked through them after we *did* meet.) Now, he still uses them but it's rare. He's not big into posting stuff online and when he does, it's all motocross related.

Honestly, I think it's attractive that Jett isn't obsessed with social media. The guys who post pictures of themselves every single day just come off as arrogant and constantly looking to get laid. It's not very attractive when a guy cares more about taking selfies than being a good boyfriend. Jett doesn't care about any of that. Just another reason why I'm so lucky.

When the bell rings, I groan. Jett wraps an arm around my shoulders and brings me in for a kiss. "You'll be okay, babe."

"I'm not so sure about that," I say, slowly moving to grab my backpack from the floor. "Every time I'm in that woman's office I consider shoving her letter opener through my skull just to end it all."

"Babe, I would be so pissed if you offed yourself in the

high school counselor's office," Jett says, laughing as we make our way through the cafeteria. "I'd have to kill myself with the same letter opener so we could come back as ghosts and haunt the high school together."

Maya's floral perfume fills the air as she goes, "Aww! That is so romantic!"

D'andre gives her a look that is both a little adoring and kind of like he's freaked out.

Once a week I have to skip my first period class to join Mrs. Albright in her office for a mandatory counseling session. After she'd first cornered me when school started and kept me hostage in her office for four hours, I haven't been able to get out of this crap. I've tried everything I can think of—pretending to be fine, pretending to be *not* fine but then making a breakthrough and getting better, lying about seeking out a real therapist to see outside of school— nothing worked. If anything, I think she has some kind of creepy fascination with my life story and she thinks that maybe she can be the one to turn me around like some kind of after school special feel-good movie. Gag me.

Two teachers watch everyone as they walk through the main hallway, so Jett just stops by the office and gives me this look. It's the grumpy, unfair look we have when we can't show any public displays of affection because an adult is watching. It's annoying and it only happens at the freaking school. Our own parents are cool with displays of affection. Hell, both sets of our parents are always all over each other anyway.

"We should be homeschooled," I whisper as I grab onto the front of his shirt and peer up into his dark blue eyes.

He grins. "It's almost the end of the first semester—you could probably just graduate early."

My brows pull together. "Is that a thing?"

He nods. "A lot of pregnant high school girls do it. Like they can graduate early in December and not have to come back after the Christmas break."

"Lucky them," I mutter. The two teachers have honed in their focus on us, so we need to break apart soon before they come over here and tell us themselves.

"Well, I'll see you during lunch," I say, releasing my hold on his shirt.

"Have fun being a desolate youth in need of intervention," he says, winking. Then he pulls me in for a quick hug before we go our separate ways. High school is so freaking overrated.

Mrs. Albright's office has transformed into a Christmas-themed oasis since I was in here last week. There are gaudy Christmas statues in front of her desk, Stockings hung on the window and even a fake cardboard fireplace on the wall. Her wax melter now has a distinct Christmas smell in it, but I can't quite place the scent. Some kind of pine mixed with a food spice.

"Good morning, Keanna," she says as I enter. Mrs. Albright's cheeks are too pink from a heavy hand of blush this morning. Usually her makeup isn't so overdone.

"You look nice," I lie. I smile and take my usual seat in front of her desk.

"Thank you, Keanna. That is quite nice of you to say." She takes a sip of her coffee and then laces her fingers together around the paper cup. "Now, what would you like to talk about today?"

It actually hadn't crossed my mind a few minutes ago with Jett, but now I have a brilliant idea.

"I'd like to talk about graduating early," I say, leaning back in my fake leather chair.

Mrs. Albright's eyes widen for a second and then she returns to that classic smile. It's the same kind of smile that the bad guy in a movie has, just before you realize you can't trust them.

"Are you feeling this way because you've spent several months here already and it's a little jarring for you, spending so much time at one school when you're used to moving around a lot?"

Ugh, *enough* with the psychoanalyzing.

"Nope," I say, putting on a cheery smile as bright as the plastic Santa on her desk. "I'm just a little sick of high school and all the pathetic crap that comes with it, and I recently heard that seniors can graduate half a year early if they have enough credits."

"Well yes, but usually those students have a plan." She waves her wrist around as she talks. "Like college classes in the fall, or some kind of problem at home that requires them, like maybe a sick or dying parent…" Now comes the pitying stare. "Keanna, honey, do you have a problem at home?"

This poor woman. She is so desperate for me to be screwed up that she's practically begging for me to admit something deep and dark. She'd probably crap herself if I actually had something good to tell her.

I shrug. "Nope. I'm just ready to get out of here and start my life."

Her eyes narrow. "I think we should discuss how you're feeling now that you've spent almost four months here at Lawson High."

"I think we should look up how many credits I have and if I qualify to graduate early."

She stares at me for a beat and when I don't relent, she

sighs. "We *could* do that, but you still have so much more to experience this year. You don't want to miss out on all of that."

"Like what? Being the weirdo who has to skip class to talk to the counselor?" I snort. "Trust me, I've been made fun of enough in my life that these little sessions only remind me even more of my screwed up past. They don't help it at all."

She actually looks offended at this. "Therapy works the best when you allow it to help you, Keanna."

"Yeah, probably," I say, glancing over at her Sponegebob themed nativity scene. "But it probably works the best when the person seeks out therapy themselves and it's not forced on them. Anyhow, let's see my credits, shall we?"

I realize I'm getting increasingly more sarcastic as I keep talking, but I don't care. Jett accidentally implanted this idea in my brain and I won't stop pursuing it until I know if it's a viable option for me or not. Sure, I'm still in sophomore biology class, but I might have enough credits. I point toward Mrs. Albright's computer. "Can you check my graduation credentials?"

Her lips press into a thin line and she continues to stare at me, either deep in thought, or maybe she's just trying to convince me to change my mind.

I put my hands on the armrests of my chair and go to

stand up. "If you can't help me, I'm sure another counselor will."

"That won't be necessary," she says, heaving a sigh. "If you insist," she says, leaving off whatever else she was going to say. She turns to her computer and types some stuff, and it could be my imagination but it feels like she's taking much longer than necessary to get the job done.

Finally, she says, "There are three types of graduation at Lawson High. The regular, recommended, and distinguished plan. You need twenty-four credits for the regular graduation, which is not recommended. The recommended plan needs twenty-eight credits and the distinguished needs thirty-two."

I wiggle my eyebrows. "So how many do I have?"

"Twenty-two and a half."

My chest falls. "So I don't have enough."

"Not at this very moment, no."

Something in the way she says it makes me wrinkle my nose. Then it hits me. Jett had said those girls graduate in December after the semester is over. "How many credits will I have in December?"

She flinches and obviously she was hoping I wouldn't ask that question. "I can't answer that accurately," she says.

"Why not?"

Her shoulders lift the slightest bit. "Because I have no idea what your current grades are, or if you'll be passing any of your classes at the end of this semester."

"So all I have to do is pass all my classes and then I'll have enough credits to graduate?"

She looks away and her lips press into a thin line. "I suppose."

Warmth floods into me as the reality of being able to graduate early hits me. That's only three and a half weeks away. This could totally happen. I could be out of here and be done with these stupid therapy sessions, the glares in the hallways from pathetic jealous girls—all of it.

"How do I graduate early?" I ask, trying to contain my excitement, which is hard because all I want to do is jump around and praise Spongebob Jesus for making this become a reality.

"You would need a parent to apply for early graduation if you are a minor—"

"I'm not," I say eagerly. "I turned eighteen a few days ago."

I glance down at my wrist, at the beautiful gold bracelet that Jett had given me for the occasion.

"Well then you'd just need to apply."

"How do I do that?"

She shakes her head. "In my professional opinion, you are not of the maturity level to graduate early, Keanna. I am recommending that you stay in school and see it through to your real graduation date in May."

Can she do this? Surely she can't do this.

"You know what? Thanks for all your help," I say, standing up and shouldering my backpack. "If you won't assist me in graduating early, I'll just have my mother come up here and do it herself."

Mrs. Albright's eyes widen and her lips press together but she doesn't say anything. I walk into the hallway and then turn back to her. "This will be our last session," I say, flashing her a smile. "Now that I'm eighteen, I won't be forced into counseling that I don't need.

I keep my head high while I walk through the hall and out into the office that leads me to the main hallway. I have no idea if I can actually call off the sessions myself, but I did and I'm going to pretend that it worked. After all, I'm officially done with this school. To Mrs. Albright's chagrin, I know I'm passing all of my classes and I will have no trouble acing the final exams in a couple of weeks. I'll have enough credits to graduate and I'll be done with this place. I don't need the *full high school experience.*

There are way better things in my life than dealing with

all this pointless drama.

Chapter 2

Jett

I can't even describe what it's like to be the newest member of Team Loco Racing. Well . . . the newest *intern*. I'm not a full member yet, but you wouldn't know it based on how much free Team Loco shit I've been given in the last few weeks. My closet has two extra feet of hangers now, all filled with the free T-shirts with their cool lightning bolt logo.

And all the craziness is just getting started. They only recently added me to their website, doing a profile and interview of me as their newest intern. My social media profiles freaking blew up after that. Five hundred new friend requests in one hour. It was insane.

Now I'm stuck going to school every day and wishing I was home so I can get back to practice. My first official race as an intern for Team Loco is in two and a half weeks at Oakcreek Motocross Park and I've been busting ass to be as fast as possible.

Too bad school keeps getting in the way. I wish it was still summer time where I could ride all day every day and make out with my girl in the afternoons.

When the last bell of the day finally rings, I head out of class and power walk until I get to Keanna. Her hand slips into mine easily and we face the throngs of people together.

"I'm so glad this day is over," she says squeezing my hand. Her hair was down and curly this morning, but now it's thrown in a messy bun on top of her head. Looks like the stresses of the day got to her, too.

"You say that like you've just finished the walk to Mordor or something." I nudge her with my shoulder.

Her tongue runs across her bottom lip in that way that usually says she's hiding a smile. "Well . . ."

"Well, what?"

She gnaws on her bottom lip and ducks under my arm as I hold open the door to the parking lot. "Well . . . I might have just completed a long journey." She blinks and shakes her head. "Well, not at this exact moment, but come Christmas break—" She chucks her thumb to the right. "I'm out. I'm done."

"Done with school?" I lift a brow. "And when did this development happen?"

Now she can't hold back her grin. "During my stupid counseling session. I'll tell you all about it later."

We're at my truck now, so we climb inside and I crank the

music. She holds my hand while we drive home, and although the sudden news of her quitting school should shock me, it doesn't. This has kind of been building for a while now, for the both of us. I know I'd fought for her to stay in school and have a senior year with me, but that was before my Team Loco deal. Now, I think I want out of school more than she does.

I pull into Keanna's driveway to drop her off, but as soon as her hand grabs the door handle I stop her.

"I need a kiss first," I say, giving her a look. "Preferably two or three."

She rolls her eyes but she's smiling. "You'll see me again in like fifteen minutes, you horn dog."

"Now you owe me five kisses," I say.

She lowers her gaze and then scoots over, leaning across the center console. The way her hand grabs my shirt and tugs me closer sends a ripple of desire coursing through me. She's normally so timid and I freaking love it when she takes control. Her lips melt into mine and our tongues graze, our mouths melting into each other.

Just when I'm about to throw her into the backseat of my truck Hulk-style, she pulls away.

"I think that makes me all paid up," she says, flashing me wink as she steps out of my truck.

I know I have a goofy ass grin on my face as I watch her walk around the front of my truck toward her front door. She turns around and mouths *I love you* and then blows me a kiss.

Damn, I love this girl.

My mom is in the living room, wearing only yoga pants and a hot pink sports bra as she works out to a kickboxing DVD. Her stomach pokes out with the baby bump from being a surrogate for best friend's baby.

"Ew, Mom," I say, just to do my duty as an annoying son. "What if I'd brought home one of my friends? Can't you wear real clothes?"

She scoffs and waves a hand at me before high-kicking along with the man on the television who is completely ripped. Talk about false advertising—no amount of kickboxing will make you look like that guy.

"I'm pregnant, Jett. None of your friends would look twice."

"All the more reason to cover up," I say, rolling my eyes as I head into the kitchen and get a snack. When I was a kid, it was kind of a big deal when my mom would dress less than mother-like. All of my friends were obsessed with her, calling her a MILF and the likes. It always grossed me out when I was growing up. She's my mom, so I didn't get what the big deal was about, but when everyone else's parents are fifteen years older than your own, your friends can't help but want to talk about it.

I'm making my second Hot Pocket when Mom walks in to refill her water cup. "Dude, when's the last time you checked the PO box?" she asks, her voice panting from the workout.

"Friday," I say. I'd had about fifty letters from fangirls who had seen the news of me joining Team Loco. "Why?"

She gulps her water and then walks over to the dining table where a garbage bag sized tote waits. The post office logo is printed on the fabric. I lift an eyebrow.

"Friday was three days ago."

She hefts the bag off the table and shoves it in my arms. "That adorable mug of yours seems to have a fan club."

In my room, I dump out the post office bag on my floor. It's mostly envelopes with girly handwriting, hearts and stars and little decorations drawn all over. Some appear to be written by guys, and if they're anything like my mail from Friday, it's teenage guys writing me for advice on how to get their own internship.

What's ridiculous is that this isn't even all of the messages. My email is blowing up as well. It was probably a terrible idea to give Team Loco our PO box address when they did my initial interview, because that's what they used for fan mail and, damn people are using it.

I grab my phone to text Keanna.

Me: I got a shit ton of fan mail. Wanna help me read it?

Keanna: You know I do. I'm gonna shower first, okay?

Me: Shower here . . .

Keanna: K. You want some of Becca's lasagna?

Me: Yesssss

It's kind of funny how I asked her to get naked and shower in my bathroom and she only said "k".

I guess part of me feels all puffed up and important as I gaze out over the mountain of fan mail. In reality, these girls don't even know me—they're writing out of a desire to get close and personal with a "famous" person. I don't feel that famous, not really. I'm just a guy who's good on a dirt bike. I guess these girls think they'll get some kind of famous themselves by knowing me? I don't know. But I do know that Keanna was into me before she knew who I was. She didn't grow up knowing my dad's name in motocross, or idolizing professional racers. She just knew me for *me*, and that's what she liked. Because of this, I trust her to be my girlfriend for the long term and I know she won't screw me over just to get something from me.

Taking one of the thicker envelopes, I rip it open. Keanna walks through my bedroom door at the exact second I slide out a handful of naked photos.

"Holy shit," I mutter, dropping them to the carpet.

She peers at them and wrinkles her nose. "Girl needs some serious razer burn gel."

I grab the photos and flip them over so we don't have to look at it, then I skim through her handwritten letter that smells like some kind of prostitute's perfume.

"She's sixteen. Are you kidding me? That shit is illegal."

Keanna nods, tossing the new outfit and towel she brought over. They land on my bed and I catch the sight of her cute purple thong and get an array of dirty thoughts floating through my mind. But then I look back at the overturned photos and scowl.

"We need to burn these," Keanna says, kicking at them with her foot. "If that girl's underage, you could definitely get in trouble."

I nod and run a hand through my hair. Is this my life now? Screening fan mail for illegal photos? "Ugh," I say.

She kneels down to my level and kisses me. "You don't need these gross photos, babe." She does a little shimmy and runs her tongue across her bottom lip. "You've got me, and that's better than photos."

Chapter 3

Keanna

I haven't always been very lucky in life, but that might be turning around. All I had to do was corner my parents in the kitchen during dinner the next day and explain to them about the pregnant teenagers.

After their initial looks of shock wore off, I told them that no, I wasn't pregnant, I just heard that pregnant seniors can graduate in December instead of waiting until May if they have enough credits. My parents were immediately on board with the idea. Becca was cool with it because she knows how much I hate going to school and Park was excited that I'd be around to work full time at The Track again, since one of their employees just quit to move out of state.

After making a few calls to the office to figure out my graduation status and set up an application, (and one call to the principal to complain about Mrs. Albright's treatment of me) Becca has all the info I'll need.

Two of my teachers agreed to let me take the final on

Friday instead of waiting one and a half more weeks until the day before Christmas break. They both essentially said that no real work is done or taught in those last two weeks so it wouldn't matter if I took the exams early.

Have I mentioned how much I love my English and History teachers?

My final exams are scheduled for Thursday and Friday mornings at six freaking a.m. since they can't interfere with school hours.

I don't care about the early hour though. I'll walk barefoot through miles of snow if it means getting out of here early and with a real high school diploma, not the shame and regret of being a dropout. And let's face it, at one point in my life I thought I'd actually end up in the dropout boat.

All of my graduation talk has sparked Jett to consider becoming homeschooled or maybe getting a GED. Of course, the second idea probably won't happen since his mom is hugely against it. I really hope he does get to become homeschooled, and it's almost entirely for selfish reasons. I can't stand the thought of Jett sitting with other girls at lunch or walking with other girls between classes. I don't think he would, but with how popular he's been lately, maybe he wouldn't exactly have a choice. Sometimes Jett is too nice for his own good.

He's been talking to his parents about homeschooling but they keep telling him to wait until the Christmas break to figure it out. I know he's angsty and annoyed about it, but I'm pretty sure they'll let him do it. All we can do until then is wait.

After dinner, I text him.

Me: Something is really wrong in my bedroom...

Jett: What is it?

Me: There's no boyfriend here...

Jett: haha. I have a shit ton of history homework but I'll be there as soon as I'm done.

I turn on my TV and stare at the phone. The good girlfriend thing to do would be to give him my blessing to take as long as he needs to get his homework done. Homework is important, after all.

But maybe I'm a terrible girlfriend because I text him something bad.

Me: Come over and I'll help you!

Jett: I'll bring cookies.

The boy gets here in record time—like, I have a feeling

he was already on his way over before I told him to come over. I hear Becca talking to him in the kitchen, so I run out to meet him. Yeah, I *run*. Like it's been years since I've seen him instead of just a couple of hours. Pathetic? Yes, but who cares.

Jett's strong arms circle around me, warming up all of my cold parts. It's especially cold in here today since Park is working from home and he always cranks the air conditioner. I bury my head in Jett's chest and he hugs me tightly to him, his hand on my head.

"You guys are ridiculous," Becca says, waving her hand at us. "I mean, Park and me were like that, too, but seeing it from the eyes of a grown up makes me want to make fun of you."

"It's not my fault your daughter is so perfect," Jett says.

Becca brightens. She always does when someone calls me her daughter without adding the word "adopted" before it.

When he pulls away I notice his dark brown hair is all messy, probably from pulling at it while working on his history assignment.

"Come on," I say, tugging on his pocket. "Let's go do that homework."

"Shall I bring the cookies?" he says, holding up a plastic

container of what looks like Bayleigh's famous chocolate chip cookies.

"Not without letting me raid them first," Becca says. She swipes three cookies and then shoos us away.

Jett and I settle onto my bed and I help him with his homework by reading all of his vocabulary words and quizzing him on them. Part of his final exam will be to know these words so I hope all of this studying will help him pass and move into homeschooling.

When we've studied until Jett knows the words before I've even read the whole definition, we finally close up the textbook.

"It's only eight-thirty but it feels so much later than that," I say, rolling over to my side to check my phone off the nightstand.

When I turn back around, Jett is laying down, his head propped up on his arm, the other hand reaching for me. I grin and roll over until we're facing each other on top of my plush comforter.

"Thank you for studying with me," he says, his voice low and sexy as hell. I slide closer to him, matching up our bodies until my toes touch the tops of his ankles.

"That might be the first time two people have actually studied instead of making out," I say. I reach up and touch his chest, letting my fingers slide down his pecs.

"Oh I have every intention of making out," Jett whispers, sliding his hand around my waist and tugging my hips closer to him. He kisses me full on, not building up to it with slow, innocent kisses. I tangle my hands into his already messy hair and shudder when his weight rolls on top of me as we make out.

This is good. We are *so* good at this. But we still haven't taken it much further and part of me wonders why. The other part of me says it doesn't matter if we take it slow, because we'll be together forever.

Jett's hips press into mine and I feel his erection, his need, both from the feel of his body and the way he kisses me. I shudder from the sensation and then pull away.

"Babe," I breathe. Jett immediately lifts up on his elbows, worry stitched across his gorgeous face.

"What's wrong?"

"Nothing," I say, shaking my head. "I was just thinking about how we haven't . . . you know . . ."

"Had sex?" He kisses me on the cheek and then locks his gaze on mine again. "I guess I've been waiting until it felt right."

"It doesn't feel right now?" I ask, trailing my fingers down his cheek.

He grabs my hand and kisses the inside of my palm. "I guess it always *feels* right. But you know what I mean." He glances toward my closed bedroom door. "Maybe when your parents aren't here . . ." His gaze turns sultry. "That'd be a terrible time to find out if you're loud in bed."

Then he winks and my cheeks are probably so red they could pass for a street light. "I agree," I say, biting the inside of my lip. "We should probably wait until we're fully alone."

"So does that mean we're ready for it?" His hand slides down my arm, leaving a trail of goosebumps on my skin.

"God, yes," I say, only to blush even more when I realize how freaking eager and dorky I just sounded.

He chuckles. "Here, roll over and I'll give you a massage so you're stress free for your exam tomorrow."

I do as he says and I close my eyes.

Best boyfriend ever.

Chapter 4

Jett

My alarm blares, nagging me over and over again as I repeatedly tell it to sleep. It's five forty-five in the morning—why the hell is it going off? I need my sleep. Sleep and I are lovers and I would like to get back to her.

Then it hits me. Keanna.

I sit up in bed and yawn, reaching for my phone. That's why I'd set the alarm—so I could send her this text.

Me: Good luck on your final exam, baby! I know you'll do great ☺

I fall back onto my bed and close my eyes as sleep beckons to me again. My phone buzzes and I read her reply.

Keanna: Thanks, hon. Now go back to sleep!

She knows me so well. I reset my alarm for the same time tomorrow when she'll be taking her second final and then I fall back asleep.

*

In just two days, everything has changed. Keanna passed both of her exams and got an A on each one. I'd known she could do it, but she apparently didn't have the same belief in herself because she had burst into tears when she got her results. Silly girl. She's so much smarter and better than she'll ever give herself credit for.

The greatest part of Keanna's early graduation though, is that it convinced my parents to let me pursue homeschooling. My dad was all for it but Mom has her reservations. She seems to think I'll spend all of my time riding my dirt bike, hanging with Keanna, and studiously ignoring my school work.

To give her credit, she might be right. But an education is important, and I do want one, so I had to convince them that homeschooling is what's best for my career. Since my parents are too busy and (according to my mom) not *teacherly* enough to homeschool me themselves, Mom found a program online that she thinks will work the best. It's an online high school diploma program, but it's partnered with the local branch of Texas State University, so I'll have an actual professor to report to and I'll take all of my exams at the college with him. The rest of the work is done online. There are even video lectures that I can watch online as if I were in a real classroom. The best part? Some of the classes will get me college credit. Awesome.

Since The Track was busy as hell this past weekend, we've all decided to go out tonight, Monday, to celebrate Keanna's graduation. So today, although I get to skip school because I'm about to drop out anyway, I'm busier than usual.

I have to shower, work one hour at The Track's front office because Mom and Becca have a baby doctor appointment, and then I have to go to the college which is an hour away and meet with my new professor. Then it's a quick trip back home, shower, and go find the prettiest flowers money can buy because I want to surprise Keanna for her early graduation. She doesn't think it's a big deal, but it is. Especially since she started school this year as a girl who had hopped around so much she really missed out on a lot of good grades in her past. I knew she was smart, and now she'll have the diploma to prove it.

I'm falling asleep at the front desk when Mom and Becca come bouncing in the doors, talking animatedly in a way that makes them look like teenagers.

"How was the doctor?" I ask.

"So perfect," Becca says, giving Mom a wide-eyed smile.

"How's the baby?"

"Also perfect," Mom says, tapping her belly. "This time we had two other couples assume we were lesbians. It's annoying how people feel the need to point out your sexual orientation when they don't even know you." Mom rolls her eyes and Becca meets me behind the font counter, relieving me of my work duties.

"I'd be damn proud to have you as my wife," Becca tells Mom.

"Hell yeah you would," Mom says, shaking her hips. "I'm a trophy wife."

"Excuse you?" Becca says, putting a hand on her hip. "*I* would be the trophy wife."

Mom throws an arm around her shoulders and flashes me a smile. "Becca, dear, you are the best trophy wife of all."

They've always been this weird. It's not a new thing. Growing up with my mom and her best friend since childhood has been fun for the most part, but sometimes they get a little *too* weird and I have to extract myself from the situation. Now that Mom's carrying Becca and Park's surrogate child, they're even closer, and I hadn't realized that was possible. It almost feels like I'll be getting a new baby brother or sister myself, since Becca is like a second mom to me.

"So, do you know if it's a boy or girl yet?" I ask.

"Not yet, but they said by our next visit they'll be able to tell." Becca logs into the computer. "But you'll all find out more at the party."

I lift any eyebrow. "Like a baby shower? Because men don't go to those things."

Mom punches me in the arm. "Men go to whatever supports the women they love, you little punk. And she's not talking about the shower. She's talking about the baby gender party!"

I check the time on my phone. I need to get out of here to make my appointment on time but I *have* to know more about this. "What is a baby gender party?"

"It's where we gather all our friends and family and reveal what the sex of the baby will be," Mom says. "Becca won't even know until the party. We're going to keep it a secret until then. It'll be a fun surprise."

I nod sarcastically. "Okay . . . ya'll are weird. . . but I love you both. I gotta go."

"Have fun at college, sweetie," Mom says, shooing me off my barstool so she can sit next to her best friend.

I wish Keanna could come with me, but she has one final meeting at the high school to get all of her graduation stuff completed. She might actually be the first girl to graduate early who isn't knocked up. Funny, because I've already heard some rumors going around that people think she must be pregnant. Those people can go screw themselves.

Why does everyone have to get into other people's business? What Keanna and I do in our relationship has nothing to do with them.

She's been right about one thing though—high school has entirely too much drama. I'm so glad we're almost officially done with it.

I crank the stereo in my truck and make the drive north to the university. I've been here before for football games, and for when Mom graduated college, but never as a potential student. It all seems a little scarier now that I'm alone. Of course, I'll never admit that. Not even to Keanna.

I follow the signs and find the Humanities building, and then make it to Mr. Walker's office. He's a younger guy than I expected, probably in his mid-thirties.

"Welcome," he says, shaking my hand. He gestures to one of the chairs in front of his desk and we sit. "So tell me why you want to be homeschooled?"

"I'm a motocross racer and I just got an important internship on a professional racing team," I say, trying not to sound too braggy but also trying to let him know this is important. "If I'm homeschooled then I can concentrate more on my career and hopefully go pro in a year or two."

"Impressive," he says, nodding. "Most kids come in here and say they're too lazy to get up in the morning, or some other crap. You actually have a good reason. How are your grades now?"

"A's and B's," I answer honestly. "I'm in advanced classes as well."

His eyebrows shoot up. What, does he think a dirt bike racer can't also be smart? "Sounds like you've got a good head on your shoulders, Mr. Adams. I'll be happy to be your homeschooling professor."

Relief hits me and I'm floating on cloud nine for the rest of the meeting. He gives me a ton of paperwork, shows me how to log into the online learning center, and tells me his expectations of the classwork. Although I'll have other teachers for certain subjects, he's the main professor who will determine if I pass or not. He's a progressive kind of guy and doesn't require too much busy work. If I understand the lesson, then that's all he needs. Awesome.

He shakes my hand again and walks me to the door. The only process left is for my parents to pay the fee and to get all the textbooks I'll need.

Mr. Walker suggests that I spend some time walking around campus to get oriented. "I may or may not get a bonus for the amount of students I refer to apply to the college their freshman year," he says, giving me a wink.

"Thanks," I say with a chuckle. "I'll definitely check it out."

I head toward the cafeteria to grab something to eat before going back home. The moment I step in line, two girls walk up to me. They're in short shorts and tank tops and don't look like they're actually taking classes, although their backpacks would suggest otherwise. Can you really dress like this in college?

"Hi there," one of them says. She's almost as tall as I am and looks like she lifts weights. "I'm a big fan."

"Me too," her friend says. This girl is shorter but still looks pretty athletic. I don't think they ride bikes though, or I would recognize them from the local motocross scene.

"Thanks," I stay, looking back up at the food menu. I already know I want a cheeseburger, but they don't know that.

"I didn't know you go to school here," the first one says. "I'm Belia, by the way, and this is Sara."

"I don't go here yet," I say. "But I'm about to start their homeschooling program to get done with high school."

"Oh my God, you're still in high school?" Belia says, putting a hand to her chest. "That is so freaking adorable."

"Um okay," I say, furrowing my eyebrows.

Sara scoffs at her friend. "Dude, she should know that. We both follow your Instagram," she says to me. She bats her eyelashes and I hold back a groan. Why does this always happen to me? Why can't girls simply say hi when they recognize me and then move on?

"So, you want to come to a party tonight? I can get you all the beer you'd like."

I take a step forward in the line, wishing the three people ahead of me would hurry the hell up so I can get out of here. "No thanks. I'm busy tonight . . . celebrating with my girlfriend."

"How old is she?" Belia asks.

"Why would that matter?" I say.

Belia smiles. "Can she buy you beer? Because I can."

"Are you really trying to put down my girlfriend based on her age?" I ask. I put my wallet back in my pocket, planning to leave and get out of dealing with these idiots.

They must see the disgust on my face because Sara gives Belia a look. "We're sorry. We didn't mean to insult your girlfriend. She can totally come to the party, too."

"Thanks, but I'll have to pass."

Sara bites her bottom lip. "Do you think maybe you'd take a selfie with us?"

I draw in a deep breath. "Sure."

The girls flock to my sides and Sara holds up her phone. I give a polite smile because this will be all over the internet and I don't want to look like a dick.

As soon as it's done, I get the cheeseburger and eat it on the way to my truck. Keanna calls.

"Hey, beautiful."

She snorts. "Why do you always answer the phone like that?"

"Because I know it makes you smile."

"Whatever . . . so yeah, I was calling to tell you something."

I unlock my truck and climb inside. "And that is?"

"I am an official graduate!" I can hear the smile in her voice.

"Awesome, babe. I'm proud of you. We'll definitely have to celebrate tonight."

"Eh, it's no big deal," she says. "I'm just happy it's over."

She can say it's no big deal all she wants, but we'll see if she's thinking differently when she gets those flowers tonight. I grin. "Can't wait to see you."

"Same here. I need to know all about your fancy college experience."

Chapter 5

KeaNNa

The most beautiful bouquet of flowers graces my vanity, filling the air with a delightful fragrance of roses while I get ready. We're all going out to dinner tonight to celebrate me graduating and Jett's transfer into homeschooling. In my old life, I would have thought having a fancy dinner with Dawn and a boyfriend's parents would have been lame and awkward. But now these people are my favorite people on earth. Jett's parents and my new parents aren't at all like normal parents. They're young and hardworking people who don't judge others and are always pleasant to be around. I wonder how much better of a person I'd be if I had been raised by Becca and Park.

I ponder the effects of some alternate reality where Becca could have children and I was her real daughter while I apply my eye makeup in front of my vanity mirror.

Tonight I'm wearing a black dress with a lace overlay that has silver sparkly sequins all over it. The sleeves come down to my elbows but the skirt stops mid-thigh so it's still sexy.

I'm keeping my hair down and just straightening it so it's sleek and simple.

My parents get a ride with Jett's parents and since we can't all fit into anyone's single car, I'm going to ride with Jett. Like I said, our parents are awesome to be around, but I still like having private moments with my boyfriend.

Jett meets me in the driveway. My parents have already walked over to the Adams' house so we're all alone.

"Damn," he says, scratching his neck. "You look hot."

Jett's wearing crisp dark jeans, black leather shoes and a gray long-sleeved button up shirt. The sleeves are rolled up his forearms, showing the sexy muscles and veins that pop out when he flexes.

"You look hotter," I say, walking up to him until our bodies are touching. He lets his hands roam down my back and to my butt.

"Maybe we should skip dinner and lock ourselves in my room instead." His voice is deep, almost a growl.

I slide my finger down the buttons on his shirt. "As much as I'd love that, this dinner is specifically to celebrate *us*."

"Okay, but you're mine as soon as we're home."

I look up into his eyes. "Deal."

*

It's still early December, but you'd think Christmas is tomorrow by the way this town decorates. I'm in awe as we drive back home in Jett's truck, the lights and decorations a beautiful backdrop to our wonderful dinner.

"I'll have to take you to the fancy neighborhoods," Jett says, reaching over and grabbing my knee while he drives. "They take decorating their houses *very* seriously."

"Awesome." I smile and put my hand on top of his.

Slowly, he wriggles his fingers under the lacy hem of my dress, and lets his hand slide up my thigh. His warmth is always a welcome touch and I try to keep a straight face as his fingers go higher and higher. When he reaches my panties, he turns his hand down and slides it between my legs, then squeezes my thigh.

All while driving.

I gasp and grit my teeth. "Such a tease," I mutter, trying to regain control of my body. Warmth spreads out in all direction from his touch.

He grins, keeping his focus on the road. "Just paying you back for all that teasing you do to me every day."

I cross my arms over my chest. "I do not tease you every *day*."

He nods. "Mhm. Just by being around me, wearing that

cute grin and smelling like a damn angel."

"You're a charmer, you know that?"

He lifts a shoulder. "You bring it out in me."

When we get home, my parents have already gone back home and are getting ready for bed. Jett's parents tell us they plan on watching a movie and we politely decline their offer to watch it with them.

Jett laces his fingers into mine as we walk up the stairs and toward his bedroom.

"You know, when it was summer I was dying for the heat to go away, and now that's it's getting colder each day, I wish it was still summer."

He snorts. "Yeah, for as hot as it is in Texas, it also gets pretty cold."

I shiver and press into him. "I wish we had a sauna or something."

He stops just inside his bedroom door. "Well . . . we do have a hot tub."

My eyes narrow. "Could we use it?"

He gives me this cocky grin. "Of course."

In the cold night air, I shiver as I pull off my clothes, revealing the yellow and green bikini I keep in Jett's pool house. "This better be hot," I say, as I walk over to the bubbling hot tub at the edge of their pool. The lights inside are turned on, LED bulbs that switch colors every few seconds.

Jett pulls off his shirt and tosses it over the back of a patio chair, the same one with my discarded clothes. He's wearing black board shorts and I can't help but watch his abs in the moonlight. He walks over to me and takes my hand. "In you go, hot stuff."

I'm shivering from the cold so badly that I don't mind stepping down into the hot tub. The warmth is an immediate welcome to fight off the cold. I sink into the bench seats against the wall and close my eyes.

"Oh my God, this is heaven."

"Not quite," Jett says, sitting next to me. He takes the waterproof remote and flips on one of the televisions that are mounted from the patio's ceiling. He turns the channel until it's on a music station and then slides his arm around my back. I'm lifted into the water and he settles me on his lap, my back pressed against his chest.

"Ah, this is better," he whispers in my ear. His hands slide around my waist and hold my hips in place in his lap while the jet streams fill the water with bubbles. Steam rises, giving the moonlit air a nice glow.

I lean back and let my head rest against his shoulder. "You never answered the main question at dinner," I say, remembering the biggest problem in my life right now.

"What's that?"

I slide my hands on top of his. "What do you want for your birthday?"

His shoulders shrug beneath me and his kisses my neck, doing a damn good job of distracting me. "I don't need anything, babe. His hands slide up my sides, cupping just underneath my bikini top. "I already have everything I want."

I gasp for a breath to steady myself. "Okay then what do you want for Christmas?"

He chuckles, kissing my neck again. "Just you."

"You already have me," I say, twisting around to kiss him. "I need present ideas . . . things that aren't me. I don't count."

His biceps flex and lifts me up again, this time turning me around to face him. I'm practically weightless in the water but it's hot anyway. I grab his shoulders and pull myself on top of his lap.

"Key, I really don't care about presents. I have everything I could ever want—there's a dirt bike track in my back yard and my girlfriend lives next door." His head tilts to the side, his hair all steamy and flattening on his forehead. "My life is literally perfect."

I frown and try not to show how much I love when he

grabs my hips and pulls me into him. My boobs press against his chest and I bite my lip, trying to stay focused. "You're getting a birthday and Christmas present from me, whether you like it or not." I press my forehead to his. "It's not fair that your birthday is on Christmas Eve."

He chuckles and kisses me, pulling my bottom lip into his teeth. His thumbs slip under the strap of my bikini bottoms and if I weren't afraid of his parents possibly walking out here, I'd rip them off.

"It is a little unfair, I guess. My parents used to let me have a birthday party in the summer to make up for it. But now I'm older and I don't really care."

I reach down and slide my hand over his erection. This time his eyes close, his head falling back to rest on the edge of the hot tub. I lean forward and kiss his neck, then I drag my tongue up the side of his ear. "I'm getting you two awesome presents this year," I whisper. "I don't care if you don't want anything."

Chapter 6

Jett

Sweat drips down my eyebrow in defiance of the chilly mid-December air. Two hours on a dirt bike, covered in fifty kinds of protective gear will do that do you. My bike rumbles underneath me, the performance racing engine begging to take off.

Team Loco gave me this bike and it's a crazy upgrade from my old racing bike, which was already a pretty fast ride. This new bike does not like idling on the starting line. It wants to haul ass, leaving nothing but upturned dirt in its wake.

It's probably close to noon by now, but we're not stopping any time soon. My first Team Loco race is at Oakcreek Motocross Park this weekend and I need to do good by their name. I need to race hard and fast and prove to them why they chose me out of hundreds of other fast guys in the nation.

And because of this, Dad is making me train my ass off.

"No pressure, son," Dad says, slapping the back of my

helmet as he stands next to me at the starting gate on our track. "But you need to shave a few seconds off your holeshot."

"Yeah, no pressure at all," I mutter, but he can't hear it beneath the roar of my bike.

The holeshot is what we call the first position after the gate drops. In motocross, all the racers line up at the starting gate and as soon as the metal bar drops, you take off, pinning the throttle as fast as you can go. The first racer around the first turn has a huge advantage in winning the race, since there's almost always a crash of multiple bikes at that first turn. If you're not fast enough to be first, then you're right in the middle and more likely to crash into a massive bike orgy. Not cool.

So I line back up, wait for Dad to drop the gate, and I pin it.

Then I line back up again, and do it all over again until Dad's stopwatch says something that satisfies him.

"I still think you could do better," Dad says half an hour later. "If you get the holeshot, the rest of the race is easy."

I pull off my helmet. "You wanna try going faster than me, old man?"

He laughs. "Don't tell me the pressure is getting to you?"

I shrug. "I'd just like to see you handle this bike and do

better than I'm doing. It's a hell of a lot harder to control something that's so damn fast."

"It can't be that much faster than your last bike," Dad says, stepping back and studying the engine as if that'll tell him what's inside of it. "I had Jake bore out your last one so it's pretty damn fast."

Jake is the best engine and suspension guy in the nation. He also happens to be one of my dad's good friends. I hop off the bike and hold the handlebar, angling it toward him.

"Give it a go if you don't believe me."

Dad smirks and takes my helmet, pulling it over his head.

He hands me the stopwatch, which is stopped at seventeen seconds. He climbs on the bike and revs the engine. "Get a good look at that number," he says, grinning beneath the helmet. "'Cause I'll beat it."

I roll my eyes and walk over to the lever that pulls the gate up and down. Dad rides my bike over to a starting line and nods.

I wait a few seconds just so he's stuck in anticipation and then I restart the stopwatch and drop the gate at the same time.

Fifteen and a half seconds fly by and Dad's at the end of the line. Son of a bitch.

I'm shaking my head when he rides back up, slamming on

the front tire brake right before hitting me. He holds out his hand and I give him the stopwatch. He just grins and hands it back to me.

"I guess there's still a few more lessons you can learn from this *old man*," he says, pulling off my helmet and handing it back.

*

When our riding session is over and every muscle in my body aches, I shower until the water runs cold. It's only two more weeks until Christmas and I know Keanna and Becca are probably still out Christmas shopping, so I take my time.

I head downstairs to get a snack and Mom corners me, hands on her hips. Her belly seems to have gotten twice the size overnight, or maybe it's because she's wearing one of Dad's shirts and it swallows her up.

"Did I do something?" I ask, holding up my hands in surrender.

She nods once and purses her lips. "You still haven't given me any good present ideas, you little punk."

I sigh and roll my eyes, walking around her to get to the fridge. "Mom, I told you I don't *need* anything."

"But what do you *want*?" She stares at me very seriously

and I know it's important to her, but I can't think of anything.

"Video games?" I say, cracking open the lid on a bottle of Gatorade. "Maybe clothes? You're good at picking them out."

"You have tons of clothes and when do you ever have time to play video games?" Mom says, sitting at the kitchen island. She opens her laptop, probably going to Amazon or another online place she likes to shop. "Your dad wants one of those new smart watches," she says, watching me intently.

I scrunch my nose. "I'd break something like that. No thanks."

She groans. "What about money?"

I shrug. "Money is always fine," I say with a laugh. "Mom, I don't need anything. Can't you take some comfort in knowing that you raised a son who is content and happy with his life and doesn't need anything else to make him happy?"

She sighs, resting her chin in her hand. "You've had a shit ton of presents underneath that tree every year of your life," she says. "I can't just stop doing that. I'm your mom and mothers don't understand the concept of not getting their kid anything for Christmas."

"How about I don't get you anything either?" I say, giving her a smirk. She glares at me.

"Oh hell no. I have a list a mile long," she says, laughing as she points toward the fridge, where I see an actual list stuck to the side with a magnet. That must have appeared today because I haven't seen it before. I make a mental note to take a picture of that with my phone next time Mom isn't in here, but for now I shrug. "You don't need anything, Mom. Your life is great."

"Oh, I'm gonna beat you," she says playfully.

I finish my Gatorade and toss the empty bottle in the recycle bin. Mom points at me as I walk away. "You better make a list yourself, or I'll have to surprise you."

When Keanna calls later, I tell her about the conversation with my mom. "It's just so annoying," I say, gripping the phone but wishing I was holding her instead. "I don't want any freaking presents, why can't she just accept that?"

"Jett," Keanna says, her voice soft. "I know it bothers you but you have to look at it from her perspective. When you love someone, you want to give them gifts. It's not like she's doing this to be mean—obviously. It probably hurts her feelings that you don't want anything. She wants to show how much she loves you and you can't fault her for that."

I get the distinct feeling that her speech isn't just about my mom's feelings. I sigh into the phone. "You're right. I'll make her a list."

"She'll like that," Keanna says.

I don't say anything, but I vow to make Keanna a list, too. I hadn't thought of Christmas and my birthday in that way before. If the people who love me want to do something nice for me, why would I stop them? My favorite part of this year will be showering Keanna with gifts, just like I did on her birthday last month. So yeah, I need to give them the same opportunity.

I guess I'm even luckier than I realized.

Chapter 7

Keanna

Now that I'm officially graduated, it feels both scary and exhilarating to be free from any kind of education until next August. Becca agreed with my plan to take time off and follow Jett around the country for his races, and in the fall I'll start college, wherever that might be.

I'll probably pick a local college for now. My parents will be paying for it so I don't exactly want to go crazy with applying to ridiculously expensive schools when all I want is a simple degree.

But for now, who cares? I'm free and my life is awesome. I'm going to run with that for as long as I can. My full time is now working at The Track, starting today.

We just opened and our first set of clients are already out on the track with Jace and Park. Jett is somewhere around here, cleaning his bike and getting things ready for the races this weekend. He's been extra nervous lately, which isn't like him. Normally he's excited for the races, but maybe that's because he's always pretty confident he'll win. I've heard enough from our clients and from Jace and Bayleigh lately to know that this weekend at Oakcreek is a big deal. Racers from all over the country have traveled down for it. Now Jett will be competing against all the Texans he already knows, plus a handful of racers he's never seen before. Maybe some of them are faster than he is. Hopefully not.

I make a fresh pot of coffee in the breakroom and fix myself a cup. The front door bell jangles, announcing the arrival of someone so I quickly press a plastic lid onto my coffee cup and rush up there.

Becca's grin is a mile wide and kind of makes her look like a creepy clown doll. I approach the front desk slowly, setting down my coffee while I eye her suspiciously.

"Why do you look like you're about to murder me and chop me into tiny pieces?"

"Morbid, much?" she says, flipping her hair over her shoulder as she brushes past me. "I am perfectly normal, *thankyouverymuch.*"

I follow her into the breakroom and watch her make a cup of coffee. "What's going on with you? Where have you been?"

She shrugs. "Oh just maternity stuff . . ." She chuckles while stirring hazelnut creamer into her coffee. "One great thing about having a surrogate is that I can have all the caffeine I want."

It hits me then, and I feel bad for forgetting. "Bayleigh just had the ultrasound, right? How'd it go?"

Becca grins and stirs her coffee like she's the evil villain in a movie. "Can't tell you," she sing-songs.

"You can't tell me the sex of the baby but surely you can tell me how it went?" I ask.

She breaks from her strict look and says, "Well, you're right. The baby is healthy and perfect! But I can't tell you if you're getting a sister or brother until the party. I don't even know myself." She's still sing-songing but I figure having your first baby is the only time it's okay to wander around in a dreamlike haze.

"I'm excited," I say, giving her a hug.

"So are you ready for the races this weekend?" Becca asks. She opens a browser on the work computer and pulls up a baby registry on Target, so she can add new items. That's pretty much all she does lately.

"Yeah, I think it'll be fun to watch a race at somewhere other than here." I pull my barstool next to hers so I can look at baby stuff over her shoulder.

"Races are a lot different than practice," Becca says, using a voice that sounds more mom-like than I've ever heard from her. "Now that Jett is in the public eye, he's going to be the talk of the races. It'll probably be hard on you at first."

My chest starts to ache. "What do you mean by that? It's not like I'm the one racing."

She nods slowly and focuses on the computer. It's almost as if she doesn't want to look at me because of what she's about to tell me next. "It's just hard on girlfriends. You'll have to stay positive no matter what. If Jett loses, he'll be pissed. He'll act like someone you don't even know."

I swallow. It's hard picturing Jett acting any differently than his usual sweet self with a happy attitude. "He won't lose," I say, but even my voice sounds shaky. "He's really good."

She smiles warmly at me and pats me on the arm. "Hopefully he'll win. He's definitely good enough."

The door jingles again and Bayleigh comes in, covered in that pregnancy glow that until now, I'd thought was just an old wives' tale. "What are we talking about, ladies?"

"I was warning Keanna on what to expect during the race this weekend," Becca says.

Bayleigh's face shifts into a quick grimace. "Ah, yeah. This'll be your first time watching him at a serious race." She walks forward and puts both of her hands on my shoulders, looking me in the eye. "Nothing is your fault. Got it?"

"Huh?" I say, lifting an eyebrow.

Bayleigh sighs and looks upward like she's trying to get her words in order. "Jett doesn't handle losing well. He might need space, or maybe a water bottle, or—" She throws her hands in the air. "Hell, I don't know. He's my kid and I don't know. He's never brought girls to the races with him before, so this is new territory."

I look from my mom to my second mom. "I think ya'll are making a big deal out of nothing," I say. "I've seen him ride tons of times. It'll be okay."

The two best friends share a look and then turn to me. "We haven't even started on the track girls."

"Track girls?" I set my phone on the desk.

Bayleigh nods. "My friend Hana's dad owns Mixon Motocross Park and she had one hell of a time dealing with those moto skanks when we were young." She rolls her eyes and Becca nods adamantly. "Jett is famous now—well, more famous than he's ever been—and the girls will be flocking around him like seagulls to a bag of Cheetos. Don't let them get to you."

I shrug it off because I'm pretty sure they're both making way too big of a deal out of this.

"So," I say, smiling and changing the subject. "Do you have any ideas on what to get Jett for his birthday and/or Christmas?"

Bayleigh laughs out loud. "Oh honey, if I knew that, I'd be using those ideas for *myself.*"

"Still nothing on his wish list, huh?" Becca says, shaking her head. "That boy is stubborn."

"Tell me about it," I say at the exact same time as Bayleigh saying the same thing. We look at each other and laugh.

"Oh, I like you," Bayleigh says, putting an arm around me. "You fit in just fine around here."

Chapter 8

Jett

Saturday morning feels like the beginning of the rest of my life. On another hand, it could also feel like the start of a short-lived dream that's about to crash and burn. I shake my head and pull on my clothes, telling myself not to think like that. It's four in the morning and we're about to head out to Oakcreek which is a couple of hours away. My first Team Loco race. I stare at myself in the mirror, my hair is all disheveled but my eyes are fierce.

Don't let it go to your head.

That's my dad's famous line, the one he's been telling me nonstop since I got my internship. The worst thing a young racer can do is get a small amount of recognition and then throw it all away thinking they're suddenly famous. I am not famous. I'm barely even worthy of news.

For now.

We all pile into Dad's truck and soon, Mom and Keanna are passed out in the large backseat.

"Girls," Dad says with a snort. He readjusts his rear-view

mirror and then focuses back on the drive.

My nerves keep me company on the long drive and by the time we arrive, unload the bikes, and get all the gear out, I'm basically no longer a human being, but just a human-shaped bundle of nervous energy. I force myself to eat and drink but I don't want to. My stomach is in knots.

Mom and Dad set up the pop-up canopy and fold out chairs and Mom insists on helping even though Dad keeps telling her pregnant ass to sit down and relax.

I'm sitting in a chair, snapping up the buckles on my boots when Keanna returns from the concession stand, holding two cups of coffee.

"That was like the longest walk of my life," she says, handing me a cup. She lifts her foot and wiggles her white sparkly flip-flop. "You should have told me to wear better shoes."

"You wouldn't have listened," I say, grinning as I sip from my coffee. It's too hot, but she's put just the right amount of sugar and cream in it, so it'll be perfect in a few minutes.

Keanna glances around, watching the other riders unpack and get set up in the pit area. We've parked near the finish line jump, right between an older guy racing in the over forty age group and a little kid racing in the peewees. I know my friends are around here somewhere, but I haven't sought them out yet. I prefer this kind of pit area when I'm at the races. As a kid, we'd park next to my friends but it's hard to concentrate like that. I'd rather be surrounded by strangers who don't bother me. That way I can keep my head focused on the race.

"This place is awesome," Keanna says. She sips from her coffee and then recoils at the temperature and sets it on the back of Dad's tailgate for safe-keeping. "It's huge."

"That's because it's a real race track," I say. My boots are buckled and I've got everything but my jersey, neck brace, and helmet on. Those things can wait until before I go ride. "The Track is just a practice facility so it's smaller. We don't need room for parking or race fans or anything."

She nods, shoving her hands into the back pockets of her cut-off jean shorts. "It's cool. I like it."

"Maybe we'll own a race track someday," I say, sipping from my coffee. I'd had a protein shake a few minutes ago, but this really hits the spot.

"I thought we were going to own The Track?" she says.

I shrug. "We could do both."

Her whole face lights up and she drags a chair over to me, sitting so that her bare knee touches my gear-covered one.

"You look hot," I say, leaning back and admiring the view. She's wearing a plain black tank top but it dips low and shows off her awesome boobs. She's also wearing a hoodie since it's a little chilly before noon. Her hair is piled up in a messy bun on top of her head, little strands of it falling all over the place. I want to reach up and brush the hair off her neck, then drag my tongue across it.

Shit, Jett. Head in the game. Head in the game.

"What was that look for?" she asks, her adorable eyebrows pulling together.

I shrug. "Just telling myself to stop thinking about how hot you are so my racing won't be affected."

She rolls her eyes but her cheeks turn a glorious shade of pink. "You're dumb."

"Dumb and in love," I say, tilting my head back and downing the coffee.

Dad rolls out my bike and sets it up on the stand. It's all clean and gorgeous—in a non-weird way—and I'm instantly in love.

"How are you feeling?" Dad asks.

"Great." I slide my hand down the leather seat. In the distance, the track announcer is telling us when practice will start. Bikes crank up from all over the pits, the different sized engines making a rumbling melody in the air.

Keanna walks over and touches the black numbers on the front of my bike. "Twenty-four?"

"Yep," I say, pulling the bike off the stand and crawling on. I motion for Dad to bring me my helmet. "Team Loco let me pick my number but if I go pro, it'll change."

Her face lights up in recognition. "Your birthday."

I nod. "Yep."

"I like it," she says, stepping back as I crank up the bike. The motor roars and I hold my helmet on top of the gas tank, motioning for her to come closer.

She leans over and I kiss her, trying not to get all caught up in how much I love this girl. Head in the game and all that.

"So this is just practice?" she says, gazing out over the track.

"Yep. So don't judge me. The best way to ride the practice session is to go nice and slow, get a feel for the track and pick the best lines."

"I would never judge you," she says, grinning as she throws her arms around me. My helmet is so bulky I can't really hug her back. She peers into my eyes. "Be careful."

I press my gloved hand up to my helmet and blow her a kiss. "Always."

Chapter 9

KEANNA

A real motocross race is almost nothing like being at The Track back at home. There, it's always busy and the air is a steady roar of dirt bike motors, but here, it's a well-organized circus. Hundreds, if not thousands of people are here and they're just the spectators. There's a ton of races ranging from little kids to guys that are over fifty years old. They even call that race "the over fifty" class.

It's crazy how busy it is, with people going all over the place and bikes riding in between everyone. I'm in awe. This is a huge race—some kind of regional race that attracts people from several states over. I hadn't been nervous for Jett's ability to win until this very moment.

Bayleigh closes the truck door and walks up to me, her lip-glossed lips turned upwards. She's wearing a boho sundress and sandals, her hair pulled in a messy ponytail that looks cute on her.

"Want to head to the bleachers?" she asks, pointing toward the set of bleachers just in front of us. They're facing the finish line jump as well and they're twice as big as the ones we have at The Track.

"Sure," I say, taking my empty coffee cup to toss in one of the big blue trash cans set up around the pit area.

Bayleigh is stopped by two different women on our short walk to the bleachers. They both want to rave and squawk about her baby bump. Both make the same adoring face when Bayleigh tells them she's being a surrogate for her best friend. It is a pretty noble thing she's doing. I know it's a little dorky, but I feel cool by comparison just hanging out with her. Bayleigh knows *everyone* here, from moms to racers to little kids and old people. She smiles and waves and calls them all by name.

Finally, we get to the bleachers and climb about halfway up, taking a seat in the middle. The starting line is toward the right, forty gates all next to each other with a break in the middle for the guy who drops the lever to start the race.

Jett is already there, in the third line from the middle. Jace stands next to him, kicking at the dirt at the front of the gate. A lot of racers or their mechanics are doing the same thing to their own lines, so I guess it's some way to help him get a better start.

A cool breeze temporarily relieves the scorching morning air and I grin, feeling my hair blow all over the place. I'll need to fix this messy bun soon.

Another woman about Bayleigh's age walks up and squeals when she sees Bayleigh. They start talking, but after a quick introduction, I turn back to the gate to watch Jett.

That's when I realize that although most of the racers have a mechanic (or dad, or in Jett's case, since it's the same person) with them, several of the guys also have a beautiful girl standing nearby.

I squint to see better and watch a gorgeous supermodel of a girl wrap her arm around a racer's back and lean up on her toes to kiss him. The racers to the left and right of Jett both have a hot girl on their arm, fawning over their dirt bike and leaning in to whisper, probably telling them good luck.

My stomach twists into knots. Those are all girlfriends, standing by their man. Jett didn't even ask me to go down there with him.

Is it because even though they're several yards away, I can tell they're all super-hot and done up like they're attending a red carpet event instead of a dirt bike race?

Is he embarrassed of me?

I look down at my crappy jean shorts, my plain tank top and my chipped toenail polish. I didn't even put on any makeup today, besides some BB cream that I used for the sun block. Ugh.

I came here expecting yet another hot as hell day of sweating and feeling sticky and gross. December in Texas doesn't really mean anything as far as the weather. I didn't bother trying to look hot. But it's clear that every other girlfriend puts their looks above comfort.

I glance around the bleachers and suddenly feel like the loser on the playground. Everyone looks nice. I look like a bum.

The gate drops and forty bikers take off, all headed toward the starting turn. Jett's bike pulls in front, barely skimming past the guys in second and third place.

If not for the big number twenty-four on his number plates, it'd be hard to tell them all apart.

Their four laps around the track take no time at all, and soon I'm standing and cheering with Bayleigh while Jett soars over the finish line jump. The checker flag is waving and he turns the bike sideways, doing a little show off move where he points straight at the crowd. At me, but it's not like anyone knows that. Even if the whole world knew that Jett Adams' girlfriend was here in the bleachers, they'd never suspect me, the plain boring slob of a girl.

We scale down the bleachers quickly, eagerly ready to get back to the truck to congratulate Jett on his win. Bayleigh grabs my hand while we walk and squeezes it. "This is really good. He'll be happy."

Jett's already back at the truck when we get there, his bike on the stand and his helmet hanging off the handlebar. I watch him pull off his jersey and toss it on the chair, his tanned skin glistening in the sunlight. The taunt muscles in his back twist as he reaches into the ice chest in the back of his truck and grabs another bottle of water.

If I could pause time and stand here, watching how sexy he is for all of eternity, I'd seriously consider pressing the button.

Instead, I settle for taking a photo on my phone. Now Jett, standing there with the sun shining behind him, chugging a bottle of water while sweat drips down his chest is immortalized forever in my phone.

Yes, please and thank you.

"Great job, babe." I go to hug him but then stop, realizing how sweaty he is.

"Thanks." He grins and throws both arms around me, holding me in a rocking bear hug. I squeal. "Gross! So sweaty!"

He just laughs and kisses me on top of the head when he finally pulls away.

I put my hands on my hips and glare at him. "Now I smell bad."

"You smell delicious as always, babe."

Jace walks up and pats his son on the back. "One down," he says, grinning from ear to ear. "Good job."

Jett nods, but I can tell it means a lot to have his dad's approval. Jace readjusts his baseball cap and glances at his watch. "Only three more to go, but you might have time for lunch if you want it."

"Three more?" I say, looking up at him. "I thought you're only racing two classes?"

"Each class races twice," Jett explains, but now I remember that I've heard that before. And although I'm excited for him to be here representing Team Loco, I am *so* ready to go home. I need to get back to our familiar little neighborhood track, where I don't have to dress like a supermodel to feel like I fit in.

Jett pulls on a white T-shirt and it's a devastation to all of womankind to hide those abs. "Wanna grab some nachos?" he asks.

I nod. "I always want nachos."

He slips his hand into mine and although it's a little sweaty, I still get butterflies in my stomach. Jett leads the way to the concession stand which is practically across the entire track. At some point our hands break free as he's caught up saying hi to other racers and shaking a ton of hands. The moment we get to the long line for nachos, I can smell them before I see them.

A flock of moto girls, decked out in pristine sweat-free cute outfits, jewelry and fancy hair. Their flirty gazes are all fixed on Jett. And they're coming straight toward us.

Chapter 10

Jett

"Ugh." Keanna's groan is kept to herself but I hear it and look over.

"Don't worry, the line usually moves fast."

"Huh?" she says, looking at me as if she's forgotten that I'm even here.

"The nachos?" I say, gesturing toward the long line in front of us. "Is that why you groaned?"

Her features soften, her gaze now peering at me as if I were a lost puppy. "No babe. I don't care about the nacho line."

"Hi Jett!" The perky voice of an adoring fan makes me turn around. Three girls around my age are all smiling so big, I'm not sure which one said hi to me.

Behind me, I hear, "That's why I groaned."

All three girls kind of look exactly the same, even though one is a brunette Hispanic girl and the other two are blonde. They must have dressed each other this morning. "Hello," I say, looking down at my wallet like I'm counting money.

"You did so great out there," the brunette says. "It was like watching a professional."

"Thanks," I say at the same time one of the blonde clones says, "He *is* a professional. He's Team Loco now."

I rub my forehead. "Well, it's an internship."

"You'll make it." The other blonde smiles. She reaches out to touch my arm, and although Keanna is standing to my side and back a little, I can practically feel the anger rolling off her in steady waves. Honestly, it's cute. She has nothing—not a damn thing—to be worried about. But I guess the moment she stops being affected by her boyfriend's attention from other girls, I'll have a problem.

It would be *kind of* fun to tell them all to screw off and make sure they know the gallon of *eu de track slut* they doused on themselves this morning is a big of a turn off, I have to maintain professional and courteous contact with all the race fans. It's part of my Team Loco contract and I am *not* going to screw it up on my first official race for them.

I take a step backward, which moves me closer up the nacho line. "Ladies, this is my girlfriend, Keanna." I put an arm around her and smile. "I didn't catch your names."

*

"That was really sweet of you," Keanna says. She studies her plastic tray of nachos and fishes out one by the smallest piece of the chip that's not covered in cheese. She's sitting on the tailgate of Dad's truck, her legs swaying in the air.

I'm sitting in a folding chair on the ground next her, but under the blue canopy. It's hot as hell, but Keanna insists that she'd rather be in the sun to work on her tan.

"What was sweet of me?" I ask, tilting my head back and eating a soggy cheese-drenched chip.

"Calling me your girlfriend in front of those fangirls." Her voice is a little softer than usual.

I snort. "What else am I supposed to call you?" I lower my voice and give it a British accent while rolling my hand as if I'm introducing her again. "Why, allow me to introduce you to Keanna, my female consort. I am in love with her and we often enjoy canoodling in bed."

She bursts out laughing and covers her mouth with her palm, making sure to keep her cheesy fingers off her face. "You know what I mean," she says once she's calmed down. "Those girls were practically supermodels and I'm just—" she looks down at her lap, her lip curling. "Ugh."

"You are *not* ugh," I say kicking out my motocross boot so it taps the bottom of her flip-flop. "You're the hottest girl here."

"Maybe in terms of temperature," she says, fanning herself with her hand. "But you should have warned me, you ass hat."

My mouth falls open. "How am I an ass hat?"

"You didn't tell me that coming to a motocross race is a fancy event," she says, eating another chip. "I look like a homeless person compared to all these other girls."

I shake my head. "You're the only girl who matters and I know how hot you are so who freaking cares what you wear?"

She sighs. "Again, thank you for saying that."

"It's the truth," I say. But it's obvious by the look on her face that she doesn't quite believe me.

*

Dad grills me while we wait at the starting line for my second race. This is the two-fifty pro class—a much tougher race than my first class this morning. I'm in here with guys in their twenties who have qualified to race a professional supercross race or two in their time. One of them, Tony Baker, has a dad more famous than my own.

Dad rests one hand on the front fender of my bike after he's tamped down the dirt in front of the wheel. "You can't let up on the holeshot this time," he says. "Do it just like we practiced."

I nod since he won't be able to hear me over my helmet and the roar of all the surrounding bikes. My heart jackhammers around in my chest. I've raced a million times in my life but only once with the Team Loco logo on the back of my jersey and on every graphic on my bike.

This is a whole new kind of nervous. Not to mention, I can't stop thinking about that weird look Keanna had on her face when I kissed her goodbye just now. She looked hurt, insulted even. But why? I had to go race and she knows that, so why did she seem like I had disappointed her?

I draw in a deep breath and try shoving those worries to the back of my mind. Emotional stresses are the last thing I need when I'm in the middle of a race. I must keep my head in the game, stay focused, and win this race.

Engines rev and I lean forward, elbows high and toes barely touching the ground. I stare at the gate until everything else around me disappears. It drops, and I pin the throttle.

Tunnel vision has me seeing only the dirt in front of me. I shift gears and lean back, letting the bike pull me into the lead. I round the first corner with other bikes nipping at my heels. There's a tire right next to me, the other rider gaining on me every second. I slide to the front of the bike, drop gears and dive into the sharp hairpin turn.

There's a loud clang of metal on metal and then I go down. Dirt fills my vision, pain rockets through my shoulder. Exhaust fumes and loud engines overtake all of my senses and for a few seconds, I only know one thing: I crashed.

Dammit.

Chapter 11

KeaNNa

I blink. *Please, please don't be Jett.* But when one of the three fallen riders jumps up, shakes himself, and grabs the number twenty-four bike, I know the worst has officially happened. Bayleigh curses under her breath but she never takes her eyes off her son.

Luckily, he doesn't appear to be hurt and he yanks his bike back upright and hops on, cranking the engine and taking off faster than any of the other guys who fell over. My heart races and anxiety consumes me as I watch him fly through the track, trying to catch up to the rest of the racers. I've never felt so hopeful and helpless at the same time.

I want him to win so bad but there's not a damn thing I can do. This is all him. The emotional rollercoaster is driving me crazy. He zooms through the track, easily passing all the guys at the back of the line. But there's thirty-something other racers and he has to catch up with every single one if he wants a chance of winning.

My bottom lip draws blood before I realize I'm biting it.

My hands hurt from being clenched into fists. A few laps go by and Jett is now in third place, gaining on second.

"Come on, come on," Bayleigh says, squinting so she can see him clearly. I force myself to take a deep breath and then I let it out slowly. This isn't the end of the world, but damn it feels like it.

Jett's bike is just inches away from the second place guy. They hit a sharp turn and Jett pins it, kicking the bike out sideways and then hauling ass through the turn, blowing past the other guy like he was sitting still.

Hell yes!

Now he just has to beat the guy in first place, but unfortunately he's pretty far ahead. They're now so fast and so far ahead, they're passing up guys who are in last place. Jett flies past one of the last place guys and charges toward first place.

The checkered flag whips through the air and Jett's bike soars over the finish line jump, simply and quickly. There's no flair to his jump this time because he's in second place. I let out the breath I'd been holding and tell myself that winning isn't everything. At least he is healthy and in one piece. Second place isn't too bad.

Bayleigh leans over, her hair wafting coconut shampoo in my direction. "Be careful. He'll be pissed." She holds up her hands and wiggles her fingers. "Kid gloves."

Jett's still on his bike when we get back to the truck. His helmet blocks any emotions on his face and he's listening to his dad, who is talking animatedly with his hands. Jett nods, and then nods again. Then he hops off the bike and practically tosses it to Jace.

I hang back, pretending to examine some T-shirts for sale in the booth a few cars down from us. In the corner of my eye, I watch him yank off his helmet, then his neck brace, then finally his jersey. Shirtless and sexy as hell, he paces the few feet of shade underneath the canopy, his hands running through his hair while he stares at the ground.

Bayleigh walks right past him and talks to Jace instead. This must be what she means when she said to use kid gloves—just ignore him completely. I study his movements as he gets a water and sinks into his chair. He's definitely disappointed but he seems a little out of it. He hasn't even looked around for me. Maybe he knows I'm staying away on purpose.

When the lady at the T-shirt booth starts looking a little annoyed that I'm not there to buy anything, I start walking slowly back to Jace's truck.

I can't stop the onslaught of self-depreciating thoughts that flow through my mind as I slowly put one foot in front of the other. If I were hotter, would he be in a better mood? If I were the kind of girlfriend he could be proud of, and I got to stand with him down on the starting gate, would he have done better? Never wrecked in the first place? The lump in my throat is unbearably huge.

Jett's sitting in the chair, elbows on his knees and his eyes watching the ground. I try not to focus on how hot his biceps are—this isn't exactly a time to be sexually objectifying him or anything.

When I'm a few steps away, he looks up slowly. His eyes catch mine and a small smile spreads across his lips.

"Hey, you," he says, his grin getting wider.

"Hey," I say, biting my bottom lip. Two seconds of silence pass but it feels like ages. I'm standing here awkwardly, wondering if I should say something about the race—some kind of trite feel-good saying about never giving up, or if I should just tell him he did good anyway, or—ugh, I don't even know.

I bet the hot motocross girls would know what to say. I bet those girls on the starting line have an entire speech of great things to tell their boyfriends after a bad race. But here I am, the dorky loser with no motivational skills whatsoever, standing with my toes curling into my flip-flops as I internally freak out over what to do.

Jett slouches down in his chair, his head tilting to the side. "Come here," he says, beckoning me with the wave of his hand.

I take a tentative step toward him, still weighing the options of saying something or keeping my mouth shut.

He holds out his hand and I reach forward to take it. Then, swiftly and like nothing is wrong, he pulls me into his lap and wraps his arms around me.

"I'm glad you're here," he whispers into my ear. "I love you."

Chapter 12

Jett

I can't prove it, but I'm pretty sure my dad made me work today just as punishment for sucking at the races two days ago. It's Monday, my first day of homeschooling, and here I am stuck at work. In the front office, no less. It's safe to say my first race for Team Loco wasn't the best of my life. I did place first overall in the first class, but the two-fifty pro class kicked my ass both times. I finished second overall after failing yet again to get the holeshot and keep it. Second place out of forty racers isn't the worst thing in the world, but it's not the best. It is *second* best.

"Absolutely!" Keanna says to a client's mother. She's working the front desk like usual and although I'm supposed to be helping her, she's cool if I work on the computer instead. I brought my laptop and set up my online profile for homeschooling through TSU. I have four classes: History, English, Geometry, Biology. They all have the same assignment for my first week. I have to write a short essay introducing myself and my skills and deficiencies in each subject.

Although I'd met with the main professor for homeschooling, each subject has a different teacher who will grade my assignments. They all filter through the main professor. It's weird, but at least it's not normal public school.

"Here's the main schedule," Keanna says to the woman. She leans over the counter and turns the paper around, pointing out various things. I'm guessing the lady is a new client because I've never seen her before. I shift my gaze back to my laptop and try to focus.

I click on the text box for my geometry class and stare at the blinking cursor. I let out a sigh. It's math class. Not writing class. Shouldn't I be able to demonstrate my skills in the subject by answering some freaking math problems?

The bells on the front door jingle and I glance up out of habit, but it was just the sound of the lady leaving. Keanna tips her head back and finishes the rest of her coffee before chucking the paper cup in the trash.

"How's the homeschool life going?" she asks, leaning over and looking at my screen. She smells like some kind of summer angel even though it's the middle of December. Her hand lotion smells like coconut and hibiscus flowers. Even in a plain black T-shirt with The Track's logo on the front, she's beautiful. Her lips are red and sparkly, and she's wearing black leggings with those fuzzy boots she saw at the mall and had to have, swearing one day it'll be cold enough to wear them. I guess that day is today.

I frown and push the side of my laptop, sliding it at an angle so she can see it better. "I have to write an essay about my skills in math."

"Blah," she says, making a gagging sound. "Want me to write it for you?"

I lift any eyebrow. "I can't ask you to do that."

"Sure you can. It'll be a trade." She wiggles her eyebrows.

"A trade for what?" I ask, reaching out and poking her in the stomach.

"You see that key over there?" she nods toward the edge of the counter where one of Becca's colorful keys with a matching girly key fob sits.

"What about it?" I ask.

"It goes to one of the bike storage stalls. There's a bunch of plastic bins in there . . . can you bring them all in here?"

"The Christmas decorations," I say, nodding. A couple years ago, my mom and Becca went to some massive Christmas shopping convention in downtown Houston and came home with enough crap to decorate the North Pole about fifty times over. The stuff they didn't keep for their houses went into bins in storage. We've never taken them out since. I cross my arms. "How do you know about that?"

Her eyes light up. "Becca told me about it and I thought it'd be fun to decorate the front office."

I know Keanna's past life wasn't especially joyful around the holidays and she's been trying to make up for things she's missed out on ever since she became an official member of the Park family.

"I'd love to," I say, grabbing the key. "But seriously, you don't have to write the essay for me. It's only three hundred words so it shouldn't be too bad."

She slides my laptop over to her side of the desk and begins typing. "I don't mind. Really."

When the decorations are all in the front office, Keanna has already finished all four of my introductory essays. I feel a little—okay, a lot—guilty for it because it quickly becomes apparent that she's done an awesome job on it. It even sounds like something I would have written, like she somehow managed to harness my personality and use it to write four boring essays.

"How are you so freaking smart?" I say, looking up from the assignment after she gives me back my computer.

She makes this little grin and lifts her shoulders. "I can't help it. I was born awesome."

I slide my arm around her back and hug her close. "How can I pay you back?"

She tilts her lips up to mine and the eager look in her eyes right before we kiss gives me a massive hard on. "No need to pay me back. We're a team."

I brush her hair behind her ear. "I'm going to marry you one day."

Her lips twist upward and then she shimmies away, eagerly taking off lids from the bins of decorations. I attempt to go back to my work, but I keep getting distracted by her perfect, perfect ass in those leggings. That kind of sexiness should be outlawed. How on earth can I ever get any work done when every dirty thought in the world keeps my sex drive alive and well?

I take a deep breath and glance up. Keanna bends over, taking strands of garland out of the bin. Then she climbs up a stepladder to hang it along the window and now her ass is eye level. I sigh and look back at the computer. This is going to be a lot harder than I thought.

Eventually, Keanna makes the front office look like a Winter Wonderland and even though I'm a guy who doesn't really care about this stuff, I think she's done a great job.

I head back to the breakroom to brew another pot of coffee for my dad who just got into his office after working with clients all morning.

I fix a cup of coffee for Keanna and me, adding extra hazelnut creamer to mine because it's so good. A few days ago, this would have been school time for me. I'd be stuck in third period, listening to some stupid lecture and daydreaming about lunch, which was the only twenty minutes of semi-freedom I got each day. Now I'm free all day, every day.

Why do people even go to normal school when they could be homeschooled?

I stop in the hallway when I hear my name said by a girly yet unfamiliar voice. Keanna's voice fills the air next.

"Excuse me?"

"Well, you know," the voice says, sounding awfully suspicious. I don't know why I stand here hidden in the hallway, other than because my intuition won't let me take another step. "Does he really have a girlfriend or is that just some rumor?"

Keanna snorts. "Does it really matter? I mean you clearly don't know him so I don't see why it matters."

"True, but my brother is about to start taking lessons here so I figure I'll have plenty of time to get to know him."

Keanna's stunned silence is my cue to move.

"Did I hear my name?" I ask, flashing my charming smile.

I hand Keanna a coffee and then kiss her on the cheek. I watch her for a beat longer than necessary, making my feelings for her known. Her cheeks flush a deep red.

"Hi," I say to the girl. She looks to be in her late twenties, which is kind of hilarious. I'm not even seventeen yet, so what the hell? "Can I help you?"

She swallows and clears her throat. "Um, nope." She adjusts her purse on her shoulder and then smiles. "Have a good day."

Keanna and I watch the woman disappear in a cloud of dust—okay maybe it wasn't that fast, but clearly she hoped it would be.

"I'm sick of being a heartthrob," I say, sipping my coffee.

"I'm sick of being the heartthrob's girlfriend." Keanna peers up at me over the top of her cup. "Maybe we should make you ugly so girls will stay away."

I pretend to be offended. "Never! This handsome face will stay handsome, *thank you very much.*"

She laughs and turns her attention back to untangling a strand of mini Christmas lights.

"Having fun?" I ask, taking another strand to help her out. "Your decorations look really good, by the way."

"Yeah and I'm just getting started. Tonight will be even more magical."

"What do you mean?" I ask.

"Tonight," she says, watching me like I should know what she's talking about.

I lift an eyebrow. "We're decorating your family's Christmas tree tonight," she says, nudging me with her elbow. "Duh."

"No one told me this." I laugh. "How come no one tells me things?

She shrugs and drapes the lights over the back of the work computer. "Maybe your mom likes me more than she likes you."

She leans over the counter, lifting up on her toes to reach the monitor. It puts her ass on display and I can't help but give it a friendly smack.

"Maybe you're right," I say, admiring the view. "Maybe you're right."

Chapter 13

KeaNNa

Christmas is only two weeks away and I still have no idea what to get Jett. Times two. Why does his birthday have to be the day before Christmas? That's twice the pressure to get him something he'll love. Ugh.

Bayleigh has a small list he wrote for her, but I can tell the items are just things he put to make her happy. ITunes gift cards, new motocross goggles, various superhero movies on Blu-ray . . . none of those are quality gifts. I need a gift that will blow him away. Times two.

When I get home from work, our house is like a magical elf gingerbread cookie house. Becca must have spent the entire day decorating. And here I thought my efforts at The Track's front office were grand.

The kitchen has Christmas themed chair covers, a candy cane tablecloth, Christmas dishes set out on display. There are lights hung over every window, every ceiling arch, and every door. The salt and pepper shakers have been replaced with Mr. and Mrs. Claus salt and pepper shakers. The cookie jar, kitchen towels, floor mats—everything has been removed and replaced with something that shouts Christmas.

"Holy crap," I say, jaw open wide as I take in the new kitchen. The decorations extend into the living room and Christmas carols play softly on our house-wide surround sound music system. Becca pokes her head out from the hallway.

"How do you like it?" she says, her expression nervous like maybe I won't be impressed. There's red and silver garland strung around her neck and she's wearing rolls of ribbon on her wrists, a pair of scissors in her hand.

"It looks amazing. I wish I was five years old again so I could really enjoy it."

She steps into the living room and does a little dance. "Woohoo! I'm glad you like it."

She pulls off a piece of garland, cuts it with her scissors, then ties the loose ends together with a red ribbon. "Next year when the baby is here, it'll be even more magical."

"I can't wait," I say, smiling as she leans over and puts the garland necklace over my head.

"I'm sorry you're too old for the real magic of it," she says, her hand touching my cheek for a second. From this close, I can see glitter in her hair, probably from hanging all the glittery wreaths that are now everywhere. "But hopefully all of these Christmas cockles will brighten your holiday anyway."

"Christmas *cockles*?" I say, lifting a brow. "I'm not sure that's a word."

"Sure it is!" She spins around, holding the garland around her neck like a feather boa. "These are the cockles!"

She winks at me and then disappears back down the hallway. She might be a little crazy, but it's the good kind of crazy.

I follow the trail of cockles down the hall and into the den, which is our formal living room that has wide bay windows that look out into the back yard.

This is where Becca has set up the Christmas tree, and it's a spectacular sight. Probably ten feet tall since the roof is extra high in this room. The tree is huge and green and covered in clear lights. All the ornaments are in boxes next to the tree, waiting to be hung.

Becca drops down to the floor and rolls out a tube of green and red metallic wrapping paper. "So what do you think?" she says, holding up a box to me.

I take it and examine it carefully. It's a fancy men's razor, electric and with its own charging/cleaning base. It looks top of the line, but it's not exactly like I'm fluent in men's shaving accessories.

"I love it," I say sarcastically, putting a hand to my chest. "Mom, you really shouldn't have . . . it's the best present ever."

She rolls her eyes and takes the box. "Obviously it's for Park, you big dork."

She positions it on the wrapping paper, then begins to wrap it up.

"I think he'll like it," I say, sitting down next to her. On the fireplace mantle across the room, three stockings are hung and one has my name on it, written in silver sequins.

"Although I am disappointed that I don't get a fancy man's razor," I say, rubbing my chin as if there were facial hair there.

She laughs. "Hopefully those will make up for it." She gestures across the room to the leather armchair that I notice is full of wrapped presents. "Whoa," I say. How many family members do you get gifts for?"

"All of them," Becca says, ripping off a piece of tape and pressing it to the package. "But those are just yours."

My jaw drops. There's at least twenty wrapped gifts of various shapes and sizes. "You're kidding? You can't get me that many presents."

Becca gives me a look that dares me to question her. "I'll

get you whatever I want to, missy, and you'll like it."

She pulls off another piece of tape and sticks it to my nose. "You *will* allow me to spoil you, kiddo."

"Yes, ma'am," I say, drawing it out like I'm a kid in trouble. But I can't stop grinning. Presents. For me. The kind Santa could never afford in my childhood.

So far I've bought her some fancy art supplies from the expensive part of the art store that she always avoids because she doesn't like to splurge on herself. But now I'm going to get her a few more things, just so she knows how much I appreciate all that she's done for me.

"It even smells like Christmas in here," I say, rocking back on my heels as I gaze about the decorated room. "I'm excited."

Becca's smile is genuine and I wonder how many years she shared Christmases in his house with Park and wished there were kids to share it with. I'm not really a kid anymore but next year the baby will be here.

"So are you coming to the Adams' house tonight to decorate the tree?"

"Oh no, honey, that's your thing."

"Why not? I don't mind."

Becca reaches for another roll of wrapping paper and I slide it to her. "Keanna, that's not what I mean. Decorating the tree is a big deal to Bayleigh." Becca's eyes glimmer as she thinks about her best friend. "It's tradition and it's for her family, which until now has been Jace and Jett. But now she's including you, and that's a big deal.

My eyes widen and Becca nods. "In Bayleigh's mind, having you help decorate the tree is her way of welcoming you to the family, officially."

"Wow," I say, biting my bottom lip as I gaze up at our own tree.

Becca nods. "And I can tell you this much: no other teenage girl has been invited over to do that at Jett's house."

My cheeks flush and Becca tosses an empty tape dispenser toward me. "Will you throw this away, hun? And then maybe do me a huge favor and get me another roll from my studio?"

"Sure thing," I say, rising and making my way up to the third floor. The entire third floor is just a small room that's Becca's art studio. It's really awesome up here, with a huge window that looks out into the yard.

I quickly find the stash of clear tape and then gaze around the room, admiring my new mother's creations. There are easels and canvasses and half-finished masterpieces set up. As I turn to go back to the narrow staircase, I get an idea. As quickly as if a wave of inspiration just crashed over me, I know.

I have the perfect gift idea for Jett's birthday.

Relief hits me hard and I feel like half a weight has been lifted off my shoulders. All of these weeks of worrying what to get him and the answer was right here above my head. Of course, the other half of the weight is my lack of a Christmas present for him, but at least half my problems are solved.

I breathe a sigh of relief and practically skip down the stairs, nearly forgetting to give Becca her tape.

One present down, one more to go.

Chapter 14

Jett

"It's here," Dad says, peering out of the front window. He's as eager as a kid on Christmas morning, and yet he's a thirty-six-year-old man and it's still a while until the big day. Every year, Dad has a Christmas tree delivered from Mr. Brown, an older guy who owns a Christmas tree farm on the other side of town. My parents took me there when I was a kid and we'd pick out trees and then bring them home, so it's a tradition. However, a few years ago, we were all so busy we couldn't go get one and when Mr. Brown offered to deliver one that he hand picked out for us, a new tradition was born.

"Come on, son," Dad says, waving for me to follow him outside.

It's already dark even though it's not quite seven yet, and the air is finally getting cold. I wish I would have put on a jacket, but it's a short walk so I suffer through it.

Dad small talks with Mr. Brown and I help unload the tree. It seems even taller than usual, no doubt because Mom wants to make our first Christmas with Keanna even more special. I swear, if we still lived in the old days where families married off their children, Mom and Becca would have made us get married by now.

Which is funny, because all of my friend's parents are constantly telling them not to settle down in high school because it's not realistic. You know what else isn't realistic? Getting knocked up in high school, marrying your first love and still being together seventeen years later. Yet my parents pulled that off pretty well, so realistic situations can kiss my ass.

Who's to say I can't be just like them? Except maybe the teen pregnancy part.

Keanna and I still haven't had sex yet. I mean, we've done just about everything else, but yeah. I shake my head and focus on the task at hand. The last thing I need to do is think about sex while moving a cold-ass tree with my dad holding onto the other end of it.

We get it set up in the living room, right in front of the window. I crawl under the bottom branches and pour water into the tree stand, making sure the bolts are extra tight.

"Nice butt!"

Keanna smirks at me when I emerge, backwards and on my hands and knees. I grin up at her and then rise to my feet. "You liked the view?"

She nods. "Mmhmm . . . very sexy."

I grab her hips and place a soft kiss on her pink-glossed lips. My parents aren't in here right now, but they will be any second, so it's best not to get too heated.

"You look beautiful," I say, stepping back to admire her red strapless dress that stops just above her knees. She's wearing a black crocheted cardigan on top of it and a strand of blinking Christmas lights around her neck.

"Nice lights," I say, touching the strand with my finger.

She grins. "Becca gave them to me. Said it was my *Christmas cockles.*"

We share a laugh at Becca's overenthusiastic holiday spirit. "Did I mention how pretty you are?" I say, taking her hand and twirling her around.

"You might have," she says, playing all coy with me.

"Here I am in sweatpants," I say, glancing down at my winter pajamas.

Keanna smirks. "Becca warned me that your mom will probably want to take pictures, so I dressed up. If I'm going to be immortalized forever in one of your mom's family photo albums, then I want to look good."

"You succeeded," I say, giving her ass a squeeze. The soft fabric of her dress makes it a little hard to get a grip. "I should go change."

Mom walks in right as Keanna bites her lip and gives me an appraising look over. "Yep. You should change."

"Jett!" Mom says, hands on hips. "This is a special night. Go put on something decent!" She waves me away and I can hear her fawning happily over Keanna's dress as I head upstairs and grab some khakis and a dark red dress shirt. I figure it'll match Keanna's dress and maybe one day our future kids will look at the pictures of tonight and know their parents were in love from the very start.

Once I'm dressed like a real person and not a hobo, we decorate the tree with my mom's insane collection of red, white, and silver ornaments. A long time ago, she picked a candy cane theme and she's stuck with it ever since. Just as Becca predicted, there are many photos taken but we all have a good time.

I watch supercross on TV with Dad while Mom and Keanna bake cookies. They had me help them with the Christmas shaped cookie cutters at first, but after it was determined that I'm terrible with anything food related, I was given permission to leave.

Now, they call be back into the kitchen and Keanna hands me an icing piping bag filled with green icing. "You can handle this," she says, flourishing her hand. "Just ice, and then use the sprinkles."

She gestures to a pile of random jars of sprinkles. I nod. "I got this. You won't be disappointed."

I wink at her and her cheeks flush. When the cookies have been decorated and half-eaten, Mom makes coffee and Dad makes a fire in the fireplace and we all gather around, chatting like some kind picture-perfect Christmas movie scene.

I'm cool with it, though. Keanna snuggles up against me while we sit on the floor, a flannel blanket pulled over us. The fire warms up the room and casts a wintery glow around the living room, shining off the ornaments on the tree.

"So what does Jett want for his birthday?" Dad says, throwing his arm around Mom's shoulders while they sit on the couch. "I heard he's being hard to shop for this year."

I hold up a finger. "I gave you a list," I say to Mom, who nods.

"He did." She turns to Dad. "We have a list, honey. It's a *boring* list, but at least it's an idea of what to get him. Keanna's gifts are already bought, since she's a girl with good taste." She flashes a wink to my girlfriend who chokes on her coffee.

"You don't need to—" Keanna says, but Mom waves a hand at her.

"Nonsense. Your gifts are already chosen." Mom's eyes sparkle from the glow of the fireplace. "You're going to love them!"

Keanna's smile is her only reply and I know she's probably a little awkward about this all, so I take over. "We got you guys awesome presents this year," I say, holding up my head. "Keanna knows you two better than you know yourselves. Well, better than I know you, at least."

Mom laughs. "Well, that's good. Jett's usually more of a 'tell me what you want' kind of guy."

"Oh you mean like how you're being to me this year?" I say sarcastically.

Mom blows a raspberry. "It's not my fault you don't want anything."

"If only he'd make a longer list," Keanna says, shaking her head. "I have one awesome gift idea, but I'm still stuck for his Christmas gift."

"Babe, you don't need to get me anything." I tell her.

Dad sips his coffee. "He's right, Key. Jett doesn't really care about gifts."

She shakes her head. "I'm still getting you something," she says, turning to look at me with an intensity that makes it feel like we're the only two people in the room.

If my parents weren't in here, I'd be inclined to let her

know *exactly* what it is I'd like from her.

There must be something in my gaze because her cheeks flush and she looks down. It would be wrong to ask for sex as a gift, right?

Yeah. Definitely.

But that doesn't stop me from thinking about how great it will be to finally make love to the girl who has my heart.

Chapter 15

Keanna

By noon on Tuesday, it's apparent it'll be a pretty slow day. While some riders like practicing in the cold weather, most of them don't. We've only had one client this morning and he had to leave early because his bike broke down right after he started riding. I like the idea of running a business that's not always ridiculously busy—it gives you time to relax and chill for a bit.

Becca and I are getting plenty of chilling done and I'm guessing this is why Bayleigh clears her throat, making me turn around. I'm at the front desk, flipping through a motocross magazine that features Jett while Becca sits next to me, working on the computer. And by working, I mean playing Solitaire.

At first I think I'm hearing things, but then the second throat-clearing makes me look back. Bayleigh's eyes are wide and she secretly motions for me to join her. She puts a finger to her lips and I know she wants me to keep this secret from Becca. O-kay . . .

"I'll be back in a second," I tell Becca, who barely notices because she's focused on her spreadsheets.

In the hallway, Bayleigh takes my hand and pulls me into her office, closing the door. "I'm taking you off front desk duty," she says, turning to dig through her purse. "As you know, this Friday is the gender reveal party."

I nod. Becca has been talking about it non-stop. They're going to announce to all their friends if the baby is a boy or girl. I think it's weird, but whatever makes her happy.

"I need your help." Bayleigh retrieves what she's looking for in her purse and hands me a silver credit card. "I need you to plan the party."

"What!" My eyes bug. "I can't do this . . . I have no idea how."

Bayleigh waves a hand at me. "Of course you do, kiddo. I've already ordered the custom cake but you do the rest, okay? If I plan it, Becca will notice and it won't be as much of a surprise. Right now she thinks we're just doing a small thing with family, but I'm inviting everyone."

Bayleigh's eyes sparkle mischievously. "Which reminds me . . . go to a craft store and get at least seventy-five invitations, the kind you can print on, and we'll make them with my printer. Also we need party decorations and stuff for seventy-five people."

My hands shake as I stare at the shiny card in my hand. "I . . . I don't know if I can do this. I've never planned a party."

"Check your phone," she says. If she's lacking faith in me, she definitely doesn't sound like it. "I sent you some Pinterest inspiration ideas," she says with a wink. Then she meets my eye and her silliness turns serious. "Honey, you'll do perfectly. I can't imagine a better way to have the party than to have Becca's first daughter plan it. I'm totally here if you need any help, but my plan is to keep her busy and occupied, pretending to plan a fake family-only party, so that when Friday comes and the real party is here, she'll be truly surprised."

"Okay," I say, standing a little straighter. I slide the credit card into my pocket. "I can do this. What's the party budget?"

"No budget. Just whatever we need, okay? Have fun with it!"

It's hard not to go completely crazy given this kind of power and the pressure that goes along with it, but Bayleigh is not only my new mother's best friend, she's Jett's mom. So I need her to keep liking me and trusting me with stuff. I need to do a good job, and screw the fact that I've never been to a real party in my life.

"I'll make you proud," I say, grinning like I'm not scared out of my mind here.

"I know you will," she says. Now slip out the back door and I'll tell Becca I have you working on the Track's mailing list flyers."

I head out the back door and look for Jett, since he didn't answer his phone. I find him in the gym, headphones blaring and two hundred pounds on the weight rack.

Great, I'm supposed to be fully concentrating on planning this party and now I have to see my boyfriend, sweaty and vascular, looking like some kind of tanned God in a tight black tank top.

"Hey good lookin'," Jett says, winking. He uses that Texas twang voice sometimes just to annoy me.

"I have a crisis," I say, sitting on the end of the weight bench.

He racks the weight bar and sits up. "You don't look very crisis-ed, so I'm guessing it's not bad?"

I heave a sigh and explain to him about the party planning.

"What is Pinterest? Mom is always talking about that."

I shake my head. "Trust me, you don't want to know right now. I have no idea how to plan a party, and when I'm freaking out, my first thought is to ask you for help but I'm betting you can't plan a party, either?"

He laughs and runs a hand through his dark, sweaty hair.

"No, ma'am. I wouldn't know the first thing."

My shoulders fall. It's not like I expected Jett to jump up and down and get excited to plan a party, but I don't have anyone else to seek for help. Jett leans over and kisses me, only letting our lips touch so I don't get all sweaty.

"But I know someone who would love to help you."

I look up. "And who is that?"

"Maya."

Maya is Jett's best friend's girlfriend and I haven't talked to her since I was still in school. She's a cheerleader and she's extra girly *and* peppy so she'd probably make an excellent party planner.

"I don't know . . . I don't want to obligate her," I say. Maya and I are friends, but not really close friends. I haven't exactly known her that long and we've always hung out with our boyfriends.

Jett shakes his head. "Nah. D'andre said she was asking for your number the other day so ya'll could hang out." His head tilts to the side. "Of course, I totally forgot to give it to him until just this second because I guess I got distracted."

A special kind of warmth floods through my chest. Maya wants to be my friend outside of school? I push Jett's arm. "Well, what are you waiting for? Give her my number!"

He laughs and gets his phone from a shelf up against the

wall. "Texting her now. I'm telling her you need to ask her advice for party stuff that way she'll get back to you soon."

"Thanks, babe," I say, throwing my arms around him. I immediately regret it because: sweat. Ew.

*

Maya comes over after school and we head straight to the party supply store, which as luck would have it, is right next to the craft store. After looking around at the stuff they have for sale, we walk across the street to Starbucks and get a coffee so we can go over Bayleigh's Pinterest ideas.

"My aunt had one of these parties," Maya says. "But instead of cake, she had cake balls and everyone had to bite into theirs at the same time. The inside was pink cake so we all knew she was having a girl."

I lift my straw to slurp off the whipped cream from the top of my Frappuccino. "Bayleigh's doing a cake, so I guess everyone will notice when they cut into it."

"This will be fun," Maya says, scrolling through Pinterest. I sent her a link to the board so we're both using our phones to look through it all. "Looks like she wants a country type theme . . . twine, mason jars, sunflowers . . . I love it."

"Yeah, that really fits Becca's style."

An idea comes to me, making me jump. "Oh my God, we should totally make her a canvas for the party..." I say while I gaze out over the coffee shop. This has the potential to be a great idea.

"You mean like her professional artwork?" Maya asks.

I nod. "Becca's Inspirations is her business and she paints inspirational quotes on canvases and decorates them to look all pretty. What if we think of a sweet quote about babies, or having children, or being a mother or something, and then make her a canvas?" Chills prickle over my arms as the idea forms in my mind, making me all excited. "It could be a party decoration and a gift."

Maya's smile stretches across her whole face. "That's a perfect idea."

We talk more about party planning and take down notes in a sparkly notebook we find in the clearance bin at the craft store. Soon, we have two baskets full of decorations that fit Bayleigh's inspiration board perfectly, and we've spent so much time together that I'm starting to feel like Maya is my new close friend, and not just the girlfriend of a friend.

"This is really fun," I say while we sort through fake sunflowers in the floral aisle. "I'm glad Jett and D'andre hooked us up."

"Totally." Maya rolls her eyes. "I love my cheer squad but those girls can be vapid and bitchy as hell. It's nice hanging out with someone who isn't a stuck up princess, ya know?"

I laugh. "I can only imagine."

Our conversation goes from crafting to boys to sex and the lack of it—she and D'andre haven't yet done it either—and before I know it, it's nearly seven in the evening.

"I'm starving," I say, as we pile our shopping bags into the trunk of my Mustang. "Want to grab something to eat?"

"I have a better idea," she says, handing me a shopping bag. "Why don't we call the boys and all go out to dinner together?"

"That sounds like a plan," I say.

I can really get on board with this concept of having true friends.

Chapter 16

Jett

A hot shower does little to soothe my aching muscles. I spent this entire week working my ass off, both in the gym and on the track. Tomorrow is another race for Team Loco and I'm determined to win.

Ironically, it can be said that I've trained my ass off for every race I've ever had, yet somehow, now that I'm sponsored and riding for an official race team, it feels like all those years of training were weak compared to now. Now, it really counts. Now I'm pushing harder than ever before. Let's just hope it pays off.

Tonight is the sex party, a hilarious name which Keanna has strictly forbidden me from saying. But I chuckle to myself as I get dressed because sex party sounds hilarious. She prefers the term "gender reveal party" but yeah, I can still laugh about it in my head.

I'm a little surprised that my mom knows the sex of the baby inside of her and she hasn't let it slip at all. Usually she's terrible at keeping secrets, but this time she's as sealed up as a bank vault.

Keanna is hoping for a boy because she has this weird issue where she doesn't want there to be two girls in the house, because she fears she may never live up to their real daughter as time goes on. She's being ridiculous if you ask me, but I've been supportive of her. I'm hoping for a boy because then I'd have a little protégé to raise up into the next massive motocross star.

Of course, if they have a girl, I'll be raising her the same way. Although motocross is mostly a male-dominated sport, the women who do race kick a ton of ass, and it'd be cool to see more of them out there. So, I guess no matter what this baby is born as, he or she will end up being a motocross superstar.

The Track's parking lot is full, as well as the Park's driveway. It's only six-thirty and the party is supposed to start at seven, but my parents and the Parks have a ton of very caring friends.

Luckily, it doesn't take me too long to find my girl. The Park's house is even more decorated for the holidays than my house, and I hadn't thought that was possible. But in the living room, they've taken out the Christmas decorations and swapped them with baby stuff. Rustic, country living type baby stuff. There are sunflowers everywhere, along with yellow and white decorations. Keanna had explained that yellow is the color you use when you don't know if a baby is a boy or a girl. Which is kind of cool, I guess, because I've always liked green and orange so I'm not sure why blue is supposed to be the main boy color but I guess some traditions never fade away.

I admire Keanna from a distance. She's wearing black leggings, teal cowboy boots and a teal oversized sweater that looks so soft I can't wait to slide my hands over it. Her hair is down and wavy and she's smiling so much it's almost like she's a whole new person. It's nice to see her having a great time with all of these people she's never even met before.

Becca sweeps in and introduces Keanna to an older couple whose names I can't remember. I think she knows them from craft fairs. Keanna smiles and shakes their hands and then the wife of the couple pulls her into a hug. I'm realizing now that this party isn't just for the unborn child that's about to be in the world, but it's also a way for Becca to show off her new daughter to everyone.

"Hey," I say, walking up behind Keanna.

She jumps a little but then smiles when she sees me. "What do you think?" she says, gesturing to the party set up. On the far wall is a decorated table with a two tier cake. It's one of those marzipan cakes that looks like something from a Dr. Seuss world. It's white with pink and blue question marks all over it.

"Everything looks awesome," I say, wrapping my arm around her waist and kissing the side of her head.

"You really think so?" she asks, her voice soft.

"Yes. It looks like one of those house design shows in here," I say, kissing her again. But I'll need to stop and keep my hands off her because if I linger too close to this beautiful girl and her intoxicating scent, I might get entirely too turned on in this room full of people.

I mean, I know it's a sex party, but it's not *that kind* of sex party. Ha.

Keanna's brows draw together. "What are you smirking about?"

I shrug. "I was thinking about the term *sex party*."

She rolls her eyes. "You are such a child."

I break my own rule and kiss her again. "Too bad you're stuck with me."

The party goes on for a while and Becca and Mom are the center of attention after everyone's been introduced to Keanna.

Finally, Mom silences the crowd by tapping a knife on her wine glass that's filled with sparkling water.

"I think it's time to get to what everyone has been waiting for," she says, throwing a smile toward her best friend.

She takes a silver handled spatula and knife and hands it to Park.

"You sure you trust me to do this?" he asks Becca. He does look a little awkward holding the cake cutting tools. He looks out at the crowd. "I'm sure you guys remember how unskilled I am at cutting cakes from our wedding day."

There's some laughter and then Becca agrees to help him.

Everyone watches excitedly as they cut into the cake. I stand behind Keanna, my hands on her hips while we watch. They make a second slice and then Park shoves the spatula under the piece of cake.

Everyone goes silent while the cake slides up and out, revealing the blue inside.

"It's a boy!" my dad says as everyone starts clapping.

Beneath my hands, Keanna is shaking from how hard she's clapping. Becca's hands go to her mouth and she starts crying and even Park looks like he might shed a tear.

Mom hugs them both and then everyone takes turns congratulating them on their new baby boy.

"Looks like you're getting a brother," I whisper into Keanna's ear.

She looks up and back at me, a grin on her face. "I wonder

what they'll name him."

"I think Jett is a great name," I say, smirking as I scratch my neck.

She grins and leans into me, then twists and wraps her arms around my waist.

"I'm really happy for them," she says softly, letting her cheek rest against my chest. Her eyes close and I run my hand down her hair, letting her take a private moment to reflect on the big news.

*

After the party, I play the role of Perfect Boyfriend and help them clean up. Mom, Becca, and Keanna say they can handle it, but us men know better. So Dad and Park and I help get everything thrown out or wrapped up and put away. There's enough leftover finger foods to snack on for a couple of days and I'm pretty psyched about that. No one loves those mini tortilla rollups as much as I do.

When Mom and Dad leave and Becca and Park retire to their room, I let my guard down and grab Keanna's hand while she walks to the fridge. I spin her around then pull her close to me, kissing her soft lips with the intensity that I've been wanting all night.

She moans as I flick my tongue across hers, and her hands claw at me, trying to bring me closer.

"Want to take this somewhere more private?" I whisper.

She gives me this perfect sex vixen grin and then hurries us to her bedroom, closing the door behind us.

This time she attacks me, pressing my back against her bedroom door while her hand slides up to my neck and holds me close.

While she kisses me, I crush my hips into hers then slide my hands over her ass and lift her in the air. She wraps her legs around me and we stay like this, making out until I'm about to explode at the seams.

I walk her to her bed then gently set her down. She doesn't untangle her legs from around me, so I crawl up her bed until her head is on her pillow and I'm hovering over her.

"Jett?" she asks, her voice soft and tentative. Her bottom lip trembles and I lean on my elbows, brushing the hair from her eyes.

"Yes?"

She averts her gaze, drops her legs to the bed. "We've been together a long time and still haven't had sex."

"Okay?" I say slowly. "I am aware of this."

She heaves a sigh and reaches up, touching my face. "I

guess I feel like now it's becoming a big deal because we haven't done it yet."

I smile. "You're overthinking this."

She shakes her head. "Am I? I mean, I want it and you want it but we just . . . *haven't*."

"We will. When the time is right." I roll over to my side and wrap her in my arms. "Of course, the time is always right as far as I'm concerned," I say with a smile in my voice.

She chuckles. "We are *not* doing it tonight."

"Why not?"

She looks up at me and presses her lips together. "Because then you'd forever get to say that the sex party ended up being a real sex party."

I can't help myself, I burst out laughing and have to cover my mouth with my fist.

She rolls over and crawls on top of me. her hair forming a wall around us. "Not. Funny." I try to force my mouth to stop smiling and the goofy attempt only makes her smile bigger.

"Soon," she says, kissing me quickly.

"Soon," I agree.

Then I wrap her in my arms and make out until we fall asleep.

Chapter 17

KeaNNa

I go to the races with a plan. I'm wearing cute shorts (that were actually sold as shorts and not just cut offs I made myself) over black tights and I wear one of Jett's hoodies with his last name and racing number on the back. Only the racers get these things, so it's pretty obvious if I'm wearing it that I'm the girlfriend.

And yes, this wardrobe choice is totally intentional.

My hair is on point and my makeup is flawless. I had to wake up at three in the morning, but it'll be worth it. I also spent a fortune on expensive shine-free, foundation and powder so I'm hoping all the walking around outside won't make me look like a swamp monster.

When it's time for him to race, he kisses me goodbye and I tell him good luck and once again he goes down to the starting line alone and once again, I sit on the bleachers watching all the other girlfriends supporting their men from the starting line. Bayleigh isn't here today because she wasn't feeling well, so it's just me here on the bleachers. I didn't realize how lonely it would be sitting here all alone, and now I'm wishing I would have asked Maya to come with me.

Jett wins his first two races and we spend the intermission together, eating nachos and watching a DVD on his laptop that we set up on a folding table under the canopy. It's a little windy today, so Jett and his dad zipped on the walls to the canopy to keep the chill out.

It also has the added benefit of keeping out the lookie-loos. Now that Jett and I can hang out inside the canvas tent between races, no girls come wandering up wanting to talk to him. No middle-aged women stare at him flirtatiously as they walk by. Nope, we're all alone.

Maybe this makes me a bad person, but I love it. I'm secure in our relationship, but I don't think any girl is a fan of seeing multiple women a day asking their boyfriend to take a picture with them.

After intermission, Jett's dad disappears somewhere with an old racing friend of his. Now that Jace isn't here to help Jett get ready, I hand him his gloves and goggles and helmet. I move the bike stand out of the way when Jett gets on his bike.

All that's left is for me to go down to the starting line with him. But I can't get the nerve to ask. I fidget and kick at the dirt while Jett gets ready. He revs the bike engine and stretches his head to the left and right.

Another racer drives by, his girlfriend riding on the back of his bike. She's wearing shorts and a T-shirt. "She must be really cold," I say.

Jett nods. "She's gonna end up with pneumonia."

I want to say: *I wonder where she's going?* Or *why is she on the back of his bike?*

Of course, I don't. I'm too chicken. But if I *did*, he'd have to answer and then maybe he'd tell me why he doesn't want me on the starting line with him.

He's not embarrassed of me, is he?

After kissing him and wishing him good luck, I make the walk over to the bleachers to watch him race. It's pretty packed today so I climb up only two rows and choose a spot without many people around.

I stare at the finish line jump while I wait for the race to start, because if I look over at the starting line, I'll see the other girlfriends and I'll get pissed.

"Jett Adams? I love him."

The voice came from somewhere to my right, so I glance over. A girl about my age nods to me. "Where'd you get that hoodie? Are they selling them at the Team Loco booth?"

I try not to look smug. "No, actually I got it from Jett."

"Seriously?" Both she and the girl next to her look impressed. "How?"

I don't know why this makes me nervous, but I tell her the truth. "Because I'm his girlfriend."

She laughs. *Laughs.* "Oh my God, you totally had me going for a minute. So, you're like his sister or something?"

I lift an eyebrow. "I'm his girlfriend. It's not a joke."

The girls look at each other and then back to me. "Honey, I'm sorry to break it to you but you're not his girlfriend." Before I can speak, she adds, "I mean, you might *think* you are . . . you could even be the flavor of the week, but—" She sucks in air through her teeth like she's genuinely sorry for what she's about to tell me. Meanwhile, my blood is boiling even in the cold air. "Real girlfriends hang out down there," she says, pointing toward the starting line.

Suddenly, I'm feeling vilified and also like fifty birds just crapped on my head.

I shrug and keep my face neutral. These girls will *not* get a reaction out of me. "I'm not really feeling well so I didn't want to walk all the way back up here after the race started." To finish the lie, I give them a polite smile. "Oh look, the races are starting!"

They seem totally uninterested with me after the gate drops, and they cheer for a lot of riders, including Jett. When he flies over the finish line in first place, I hop off the bleachers and book it back to our truck, squeezing my hands into fists in an effort to calm down. I should really just woman up and ask him why he won't let me go down to the starting line with him.

There's one race left of the day, so there's still time to secure my rightful place at his side. I just need the metaphorical balls to ask him.

Jett's already back at the truck when I get there, and so is Jace. His dad is beaming with the third win of the day, and Jett's in a great mood as well.

He gives me that sexy grin when I approach. His arms open and I jump into them, wrapping him in a bear hug. "I'm proud of you babe, you did awesome."

He nods and kisses me. With the cooler air, he's not as sweaty after a race. "One more win and I'll have kicked this day's ass."

"Hey-hey! My man!"

I release my boyfriend as a group of Team Loco guys walk up and loudly congratulate Jett on his win. They stand outside of our walled canopy so there's no getting rid of them for a while. Jett introduces me to the guys as his girlfriend and I kind of wish those girls from the bleachers were here to witness it.

Jace offers me a hot chocolate while the guys are still talking and I spend some time talking with him while I wait to get my boyfriend back. He really is a cool dad and he seems to like having me around.

And then, just like always—like freaking clockwork—a girl walks up all pink-cheeked and grinning from ear to ear. She asks Jett to take a picture with her. After she leaves, a few more girls do the same thing, but they're all about twelve years old so it doesn't bother me much.

Jace and I talk about Christmas and I give him advice on what to get his wife besides the comfortable pajamas she asked for. The Team Loco guys *finally* say their goodbyes and wish him luck on his last race of the day. As soon as they're out of earshot, I go over to Jett and take his hand.

"If we get home in time, do you think we could get Mexican food for dinner?" I ask.

His eyes go wide. "Oh hell yes, that would be so good. Way better than concession stand nachos."

"Dude, don't knock the nachos," I say, pretend punching him. "Those things are the sole reason I wake up at the butt-crack of dawn and come to the races with you.

"Oh, that hurts, Key." Jett grips his heart and pretends to be in tremendous pain.

"Hi there!" a soft voice says from a few feet away.

Another, more high-pitched voice says, "That was a nice win, Jett."

Jett gives me this sad smile and we both turn to face the three gorgeous women in their twenties who are approaching us. One of them, an Indian woman with long perfect hair, winks and waves at Jace, who clears his throat and then walks back into the canopy.

"We're huge fans," one of them says. I'm not really paying attention anymore. I walk over to the tailgate of Jace's truck and pull myself up to sit on it while Jett does his thing with his adoring fans.

They gush and smile and tell him how great he is and he takes it all in stride. Then, of course, the cell phones come out and one by one, Jett takes their phones and holds it out for a selfie.

One girl throws her hand around his shoulder. It's annoying, yeah, but I know where his heart belongs.

Just before he snaps the final photo, he glances over and gives me a wink. And this might be the first time in the history of the world that a guy has managed to melt someone's heart while being embraced by three other girls.

Chapter 18

Jett

The morning after race day, I lie awake in bed, still plagued by the bad feeling about Keanna. Yesterday was weird. On the surface, it was a great day because I won all my races and did a spectacular job representing Team Loco. Keanna and I didn't fight, or argue, or have anything wrong happen . . . so why does it feel like she's upset with me?

I fell asleep worrying about this after talking with her on the phone all night. She didn't seem mad at me, but things felt off and I'm not sure why. I guess I hoped that when I woke up today, I'd feel better.

Well, I don't.

It's Sunday and The Track is closed. Tomorrow is the start of the last week of school before Christmas break so it'll be a slow week and then we'll have the pre-Christmas lock-in and it'll be busy as hell.

My homeschooling is going okay. It's only been a week but so far all of my online teachers enjoyed my (well— Keanna's) introductory essay. So far I've just had one easy assignment per day for each class.

Easy peasy.

The hard part is dealing with this concern over Keanna. How can you fix a problem with your girlfriend when you're not even sure if there is a problem? Is it all in my head?

Maybe she's worried about my birthday and Christmas coming up because I know she doesn't want to get me anything on the list I made for my mom. I wish I could convince her that I don't need or want anything as long as she's by my side. She's all I need and no amount of fancy gifts could ever replace her.

In an effort to make things feel normal for us again, I call her to ask her on a date. Living next door and working with each other is a great way to fall into a boring routine of a relationship and I don't want that to happen to us. My parents always make time for date nights because it's important, and I'm going to do the same thing.

She sounds sleepy when she answers the phone. I glance at the clock. It's eleven in the morning.

"Hey, beautiful."

She chuckles and then yawns. "What's up?"

"I wanted to ask you on a date tonight. Dinner and a movie?"

"That sounds awesome," she says, her voice perking up. I

can hear her smile through her words. "That new superhero movie is out and we haven't seen it yet."

"Perfect. I was thinking of going to The Spot for dinner. It's this really good seafood place and a couple of days ago you said you wanted coconut shrimp so I thought it'd be great."

"Yum," she says. It sounds like she's still in bed, maybe stretching out her arms. I really wish I was in that bed with her. "But, Jett?" she asks.

My chest constricts. "Yes?"

"Can we go out for lunch instead of dinner?"

"But dinner is more of a romantic time for a date."

She laughs. "Babe! I don't want to wait until later. I want to see you now."

I grin. "Guess I can't argue with that."

*

We opt to see the movie first since we're both not that hungry yet. I hold open doors and keep my arm around her, doing everything I can think of to be romantic. I need her to know that things between us are perfect.

She may be smiling on the outside but something feels wrong ever since the races yesterday. I *need* things to get better.

The armrests in the theater lift up, so Keanna snuggles against my chest while we watch the movie. I love the feeling of her leaning on me, like she can count on me. Like I make her safe.

After the movie, we head to The Spot, a kitschy restaurant, the kind with tons of crap all over the walls and big fake fish hanging from the ceiling. The décor may be annoying, but their food is good.

We order fried pickles for an appetizer and Keanna gets her coconut shrimp, which puts a genuine smile on her face.

"This is the best coconut shrimp in the world," Keanna says, holding up the tail of the piece she just ate. "I am in love."

I nod and reach for one of my fried shrimp. "This place is really good. They only use locally caught seafood as well, so it's not that frozen shit."

My phone buzzes so many times it makes both of us look toward my pocket. I pull it out just enough to see the screen. "Social media alerts," I say, rolling my eyes.

This usually happens when a magazine or website posts a new article about me. Suddenly, I'll get fifty billion comment and post alerts from fans talking to me or about me. I slide the phone back in my pocket and reach for another fried pickle. These things are pretty good.

Keanna makes this big dramatic sigh. "My boyfriend is so popular," she says, grinning. "I feel like I should become a movie star or something so you can get a taste of what it's like to date someone so famous."

I take a bite of shrimp and peer at her for a long moment. "I don't see it. You're not really the actress type . . . I see you as more of the person who designs the movie sets."

"Is that supposed to be a compliment?" she asks, but she doesn't seem offended or anything.

I nod. "You're artistic. You did a great job on the party decorations and I think you'd bring a movie to life, ya know?"

"That's really sweet," she says, grabbing my hand from across the table.

For the first time since the races, I'm starting to feel like maybe things are okay again. Looks like my romance paid off.

After lunch, we walk out onto the restaurant's patio. It's a vast deck on a marina, so we can walk for a long ways and look at the water and the boats passing by. In the center of the deck is a circular viewing area. Signs identify the several types of fish in the viewing area, and there's even a vending machine to get a cup of fish food to feed them.

Keanna's eyes light up. "Do we have any quarters?" she says, digging through her purse. She comes up with one quarter but there's a money changing machine next to the food so I use two dollar bills from my wallet to get more.

We have a blast dropping pellets of fish food down to the fish, and soon there's dozens of them all floating around the water, begging for the next piece of food.

Keanna tosses a piece toward an empty section of water and we watch a fish swim toward it, only to have another catfish beat him to it.

"Rude!" Keanna says, tossing more pieces down the fish who got left out.

A little kid walks up with his grandmother, who tells him she doesn't have any quarters. Keanna gives him some of ours and it melts my heart to watch the kid's face light up excitedly. I love that she's kind and generous and not some stuck up motocross groupie like many girls I've known before.

Keanna excuses herself to go to the restroom back inside the restaurant and I stay, feeding the fish with the little boy.

My phone keeps buzzing like crazy, so once my cup is out of food, I decide to check the messages. But I barely type in my lock code when someone approaches me. It's a girl around my age, pretty but with something sly behind her eyes. I instantly know she's the kind of girl who can't be trusted, and even if I were single, I'd know to stay away from this one.

"Hi there," she says, dropping a quarter into the machine and letting it fill up her plastic cup. "Are the fish hungry today?"

"Yeah, they're gluttons," I say, turning back around and smiling at the little boy who is still feeding the fish.

"I can't believe I ran into someone famous while at the marina," she says, not looking at me as she strides up to where I'm standing near the fish viewing area. Ugh.

Of course.

Why can't I ever be approached by normal people? People who *don't* know who I am.

"I'm not famous," I say, using the same old line I've said many times before.

She snorts. "don't worry, I'm not some crazy stalker fangirl or anything."

Yeah, right, like I trust you. Instead, I say, "Good. I've had enough of those in my lifetime."

She turns to me and gives me what can only be described as a sultry, *come-hook-up-with-me* smile.

"Nice meeting you," I say, pushing off from the railing. "I need to get back to my girlfriend."

"You already have a new girlfriend?" she says, her voice higher than before. "Damn, that was fast. Like, super-fast."

I stop. I should probably keep leaving but dammit, now I'm curious. "We've been dating a while," I say. "What do you mean by *fast*?"

She peers at me like she's trying to tell if I'm lying. "The internet says you're single now."

"When did it say that?" I shouldn't care, but I ask anyway.

She lifts a shoulder and tosses more food to the fish. "Today."

So that's what all those phone alerts were about. I put on a casual smile. "You can't believe everything you read online, unfortunately. My girlfriend and I are still very much together."

"Weird," she says. She flips her hair over her shoulders. "Well, good thing I'm not one of your stalker fangirls or I might be disappointed."

I nod once and head back toward the restaurant. I see Keanna walking toward me, weaving her way through the dozens of outdoor tables. She gives me a cute little wave and I wave back, walking quicker to meet her sooner.

"What's that look about?" Keanna says, eyeing me suspiciously when we're finally back together, my hand in hers.

"Oh, nothing," I say, letting out a long sigh.

As we head back to the truck, I remember a speech my dad gave me a while back. It was before I'd met Keanna but when I was still fast enough and winning enough races to get noticed on a more popular level. He'd told me that dating and motocross don't mix well. That fame changes a person, makes them more powerful because they can date nearly anyone they want. He said girls can't handle the jealousy and competition and guys let it get to their head too easily. I'd been warned that dating and fame are hard to manage, and yet I'd thrown away all those warnings when I met Keanna.

Dad's advice doesn't hold true to some aspects of dating and fame—I don't care to play the field anymore. I only want Keanna and she only wants me. But he was right about one thing. It's not easy. I don't like having the public analyze my personal life outside of the races. I don't like getting hit on by girls of all ages, some of whom could be my mother, or grandmother, for that matter.

Dad didn't go back to professional motocross after falling for my mom. Although being a racer has been my dream for as long as I can remember, maybe it's not worth it in the long run. Dreams can change, after all. For now, I guess I'll see what happens.

Chapter 19

KEANNA

Since it's a slow week at work, I get permission to come in at noon instead of at eight in the morning. Jett has been doing all of his homeschool work in the mornings, so this is the perfect time to work on my present for him.

With only a few hours of headache trying to make our home printer work, I managed to take my favorite photo of Jett, blow it up into nine pieces of paper, and print it out on canvas transfer papers I found at the craft store.

Then, I got a stretched canvas from the art section that's the exact size of my blown up image. Using internet tutorial videos, I place all nine sheets of transfer paper onto the canvas and then scrape it with a spatula until the image transfers over.

I hold my breath as I peel off the papers, hoping that the canvas image looks as good as it is in my head.

It comes out perfectly. I'm grinning so much as I look over the canvas. Now, my photo of Jett, muscular and shirtless, standing next to his dirt bike, is a work of art.

I stand back and admire my work. But it's not done yet.

My plan is to decorate it with a painted on quote and then seal it up with some of Becca's clear sealant. That way it'll be waterproof and last forever.

At first I think I'm imagining Jett's voice but then I hear it again. He calls my name.

He's in the house!

"Keanna? Are you upstairs?"

Shit. I rush to move the canvas to the corner of the room and then I take a sheet and toss it over.

"I'll be right down!" I call out, nearly tripping over Becca's art supplies as I scramble to the doorway. I pull it open just as Jett starts up the stairs to the studio.

"Hey," I say, taking a deep breath and trying to look normal. If he gets suspicious of what I'm doing up here he might figure out that I'm planning something for him.

"Done with your school work already?" I say, putting a hand on my hip. If I change the subject, then maybe he won't ask what I was doing.

"Nope." Even from his position at the bottom of the stairs, he looks tall and handsome as hell. "I skipped out on the last assignment because I wanted to see you."

I hold onto the handrail and step down until I'm two steps higher than he is. "That's very bad of you, Jett Adams.

I might have to punish you."

He grins. "I think I need a paddling."

He holds out his arms and I jump into them, holding on when he grabs me and heads back to my room. Since my parents aren't here, I don't hold back the squeals when he drops me to the bed and tickles me.

"Stop!" I gasp, squirming to get out of his wiggling fingers. He dives onto the bed next to me and I seize my opportunity to tickle him right on the side of his ribs.

"Hey now! Not fair!" Jett says, rolling out of the way. "I can only tickle you. You can't tickle me."

I roll over onto my stomach and prop myself up on my elbows. "What kind of double standard is that?"

He fluffs the pillow next to mine and lays down. "It's a double standard that works in my favor."

I roll my eyes. "Dork."

It's past noon and Jett's still in his flannel Homer Simpson pajama pants and a black undershirt. I guess he really did come over because he wanted to see me.

"I have to go to work soon," I say, frowning.

"I know. That's why I wanted a few minutes with you." He tucks his hands behind his head and stares at the ceiling. "Plus, we need to talk."

Those formidable words are usually a sign of bad news

but the way he says them makes me more curious than worried. "What's up?"

"There's some dumbass rumor online that Jett Adams is a single man again."

He looks over at me, searching my eyes for something.

I shrug. "So?"

"It's no big deal because obviously we're fine, but it's annoying."

"Are you going to say anything or just let it go?" I ask.

He looks over and leans up on his elbow. "I have an idea, but you'd have to go along with it."

"Oooh, enticing." I wiggle my eyebrows. "What is it?"

He sits up and gnaws on his bottom lip. "Okay, it's kind of stupid. Like—way stupid. This isn't my usual personality at all."

I narrow my eyes at him. "Does it involve social media?"

"Yep."

I sit up, eager to hear about his *so-not-like-him* plan. "You want me to type up a message that tells everyone you're happily dating me and post it to your account?"

He shakes his head, and takes out his cell phone. "I have a better idea. Let's take some selfies."

I make this exaggerated gasp and cover my mouth with my fingers. "*Selfies*? You? Wow, I am shocked."

He laughs and shakes his head. "I know. I'm not a selfie person. But I was thinking, instead of addressing the stupid rumors by telling everyone I'm not single, what if I post a picture of us in bed and send it to Instagram with a caption that says I'm sleeping in with my girl or something? That way it's like a subtle *fuck you* to the people starting rumors."

I grin. I really like his ideas when they involve me. "That's a perfect plan." I take his phone and open the camera. "But take off your shirt."

He lifts an eyebrow and I wave my hand for him to get on with it. "Take it off. It'll look more convincing." Then I run my tongue across my lip. "Plus I just want to see how freaking sexy you are before I go to work."

"Can't say no to that," Jett says, lifting up and pulling off his undershirt. He tosses it to the floor and then lays down in bed, beckoning me into his shoulder. I lean against him and then spend way too much time fixing my hair and trying to look extra cute for a picture that's supposedly taken just when we woke up.

He holds out the camera, we give sexy but sleepy smiles, and he snaps the photo. I enjoy the smell of his cologne as I snuggle against him, watching him upload the photo to Instagram.

He types *I love lazy days with my girl* and puts a heart

emoji next to it. I try not to be a vain person, but seeing the picture of us on his Instagram account that has fifty thousand followers kind of makes my whole day.

"You're the coolest girlfriend ever," Jett says after he puts his phone on my nightstand. "I tell you the internet is saying we broke up and you don't even care."

I shrug and run my fingers down his bare chest. I would kill to have half the tanned and toned body he has. "Who cares about rumors? It's not like we know any of those people."

"True," he says, kissing my forehead. "So . . . this is a sexy outfit you're wearing."

I look down. I chose a pair of leggings that are a little too tight and a spaghetti strap pink tank top that I'm not too fond of, that way if any paint or glaze got on it, it wouldn't be a huge loss. Jett slips his finger under the strap and pushes it down my shoulder. He leans over me and kisses the skin where his fingers touched. I close my eyes and revel in his gentle embrace, the soft touch of his lips on my collarbone.

Warm hands slide down to my hips and then his fingers slip under my tank top.

The fabric rises until my breasts are exposed and Jett hovers over me, kissing me while his chest presses against mine. I moan from the intensity of his kiss and then lean back, letting him pull off my shirt. He tosses it right on top of his on the floor and then our tongues caress each other while his hands roam down my body.

I grab his back and pull him into me, feeling his excitement press into my stomach.

When he reaches for my leggings, I beat him to it. I can't help myself, he's so hot and I want him so badly. I slip the leggings down to my angles and then kick them off, leaving everything exposed except for what's under my panties.

Jett's eyes fill with desire, and he grabs my hips, crushing me against him while we make out. I tangle my hands up in his hair, breathing hard against his neck.

He is so sexy and I want him so bad.

Chapter 20

Jett

The way she moves beneath me, her fingernails digging into my back—it's all too much to experience and still walk away. I let my fingers explore her body, but focus on kissing, wondering if just making out will be enough.

"Jett," she whispers, gasping for air. Her hands dig into my hair. "It's time."

"Are you sure?" I ask, pulling back to look into her eyes.

She pulls at my pajama pants. "Yes, I'm sure."

I stand up and although I don't want to leave her, I rush over and lock her bedroom door. Her parents won't be home anytime soon but I am *not* about to get caught in bed with their daughter. That would be embarrassing and fifty kinds of traumatizing.

When I walk back to her bed, she gives me a sultry gaze and wiggles out of her panties. I take in a deep breath and drop my pants to the floor.

"Are you sure?" I ask, not getting back in bed until I know this is okay.

She nods eagerly and waves for me to join her. "Stop stalling," she whines. "You're just being mean now."

"Never," I say, crawling into bed with her. We slip under her sheets and I tug them up around us, knowing it'll help ease the awkwardness if everything isn't on display.

Besides, I have the rest of my life to admire her perfect body. Right now it's all about us.

I pull her face toward mine, and kiss her with everything that I have. Her back arches toward me and I stop, suddenly remembering something very important.

"You said you were on the pill, right?"

"Yep," she says, lifting her head and kissing my shoulder, then my neck. "Take it at the same time every day. You've seen me."

I nod. That's true. I take a deep breath and relax into her embrace, allowing myself to love her in the way I've been wanting to since the day I met her.

Her green apple shampoo smells like heaven when I bury my face into her neck. I let myself enjoy every touch, every sharp gasp of breath, the cute little way she shudders underneath me.

Despite my best efforts, it doesn't last very long, but she doesn't seem disappointed. After, we cuddle in her bed, her fingers tracing soft circles on my chest.

"That was better than I imagined," she breathes, her breath tickling my shoulder.

I run a hand through her hair. "And exactly how many times have you imagined that?"

She giggles into my neck and shakes her head. "*So* not telling you."

I take a deep breath and let it out slowly, reveling in the feel of her in my arms, the way the sun shines through the windows on this perfect winter day.

"I like this," I whisper, kissing the top of her head.

"You know what I like the most?" she says, looking up at me. "It just happened."

I lift an eyebrow. "*That's* what you liked the most?"

"Yeah, it was just us. Just a thing. After all these months of me stressing about it like some kind of crazy person, we finally did it." She draws in a deep breath and lets it out slowly. "All of that talk for waiting for the perfect time . . . and it turns out *this* was the perfect time."

She smiles up at me and I lean down and kiss her forehead. "It was perfect."

"And now that it's over, we can start doing it all the time," she says playfully.

"Oh yeah?" I run my finger up her side, feeling goosebumps lift on her skin. "That sounds like a great way to never get any more school work or riding done."

She frowns in this silly way. "I guess we'll just have to stay in this bed forever."

I close my eyes and wrap my arms tightly around her. "Sounds like a plan to me."

We rest in each other's arms for a while and just when I'm about to doze off, I hear her sigh.

"Seriously, Jett. *How* did I live so long without experiencing that?"

"It was that good, huh?"

She shrugs. "There's something special about being with someone you love. I guess I never realized how special it really is."

I sit up and pull on my clothes, handing hers back to her. It's been an hour or so and we don't want to risk any awkward family encounters.

"It was also awesome in other ways," I say, sitting back on her bed.

She tugs her shirt back over her head. "How so?"

I'm not sure I want to tell her for fear of sounding like some kind of perv. "Well ... we ..." I make these God-awful gestures with my hands, but it doesn't help explain anything. "It was a first for me, uh—physically speaking."

She gives me exactly the kind of crazy look I deserve.

"Huh?"

I sigh. "No condoms. That was . . . intense."

Her confusion turns to desire. "Oh yeah?" she leans forward on her hands, pressing her boobs together between her arms. "You liked that?"

I nod eagerly. "Oh yeah. Way more than I should have."

"Good," she says, grinning so hard her eyes crinkle. "I like knowing I could give you something no one else has."

"Oh, you have. You *definitely* have."

Even her neck blushes with the way I look at her. It makes me want to go for round two. Instead, I check my phone, which has now blown up with notifications from my newest picture post.

"Wanna see?" I ask her, waving my phone.

"Hell yes," she says, snatching it from my grasp. She falls back on her bed and holds the phone so we can both see.

OHEMGEE, HE STILL HAS A GIRLFRIEND
Wait, is that the same girl or what?
I'm going to cry myself to sleep again. Dammit, I hate everything my life is shit.

"Wow, I feel bad for that girl," Keanna says after reading the third comment. "Maybe you should reply to her and say her life isn't shit.

I shake my head. "I've been advised against that by a few of my Team Loco racing buddies. Apparently interacting with the hyperactive fans is a way to get a stalker. Or, even worse, if you talk to them and then don't keep replying they might threaten suicide and then you have to get the cops involved."

I run a hand through my hair, remembering the story one of the guys told me during my first Team Loco race. He's had to call the police on three different internet girls who had obsessively written him and said they'd kill themselves if he didn't reply. Fearing for their safety, he kept talking to them and it all got really crazy. One of the girls even found out where he lived and broke into his house. I shudder at the memory. I do *not* want that to happen to me.

"Wow." Keanna's lips form a small O. "That's some scary stuff. I say we make you ugly and gross so no one likes you."

I cross my arms. "I don't like that idea."

She laughs and hands my phone back to me. "Fine, stay sexy. I like you better that way anyhow." She takes her sweet time crawling out of bed, giving me a view of her ass in those tight leggings. "I guess I should get to work now," she says, slipping into her closet.

"Fine," I say, sinking back in her bed. "I'll be waiting right here for you to get back."

*

By Friday, I can't concentrate on helping Dad train our five-year-old clients. Sure, I'm dressed appropriately, I'm standing out on the track in the sun, and I'm even helping kids start their bikes. My body and brain are here at work—but my mind is elsewhere.

Yep, I am lost in a vortex of daydreaming about a beautiful girl with dark brown hair and even darker eyes. Her soft skin, the way she giggles when I shower her with kisses. I am totally and completely consumed by Keanna Park.

It royally sucks that I'm stuck at work.

Somehow, I manage to fake like I'm actually paying attention all day and when my shift is almost over, D'andre shows up at The Track, but he's not in his riding hear.

"Hey man," he says, fist-bumping me. "What do you got planned after this?"

I shrug. The answer is Keanna, obviously, but I'm a guy and I have to pretend like I'm not totally lost to my friends.

"Cool, so you wanna hit up the mall or something?" He takes out his wallet and flips through some twenty dollar bills. "I have two hundred and seven dollars and need to find a Christmas present for Maya."

Damn. I need to get Keanna's present, too, and the longer I wait, the more hectic and horrifically busy the mall will be. I really should go now, but sacrificing a few hours away from my gorgeous girlfriend is going to suck.

"Yeah, sounds good," I say, choosing the logical thing over what my heart wants to do. "I'll meet you in the parking lot in a minute."

I head inside and clock out, then call Keanna and tell her the plan.

"That works," she says, not even sounding disappointed. "I'm actually kinda busy so take your time."

"Cool," I say, even though I don't believe it. "I'm gonna miss you."

"I always miss you," she says, and then she kisses the phone. "Love you."

"Love you more."

At the mall, I find about five thousand things I know Keanna would love. I don't buy them all because that would make me a crazy person, plus I've seen half the stuff my mom got her already and I'm not sure Keanna's bedroom is big enough to house it all.

I get her favorite body lotion from Victoria's Secret, and

then throw in a gift card just because.

D'andre goes a little overboard in the same store. He gets Maya three bras that apparently she has already picked out and hinted for. I think it's a little weird getting a girl a bra, but whatever.

I get a few smaller things throughout the store, mostly just stuff that makes me think of her, like a new phone case that's solid pink glitter. But I'm still missing the main gift. The big, awesome, present that will make her mouth drop and her eyes water.

The kind of gift that says I'm the best boyfriend on earth.

I'm about to give up hope on finding such a perfect gift, but then we stop to get some fish tacos and a shiny display case around the corner catches my eye.

While waiting for our food, I walk over and gaze at the beautiful items beneath the glass. And I know. As sure as I've known anything, that this is the perfect gift for Keanna.

Chapter 21

KeaNNa

It's extra windy today, as evidenced by the creaking and whipping sound on the studio's windows. On the third floor, I almost feel sea sick when I look outside and see all of the trees swaying like crazy in the breeze. Of course, the house is sturdy so I'm not really moving. Maybe I've just been breathing in this clear sealant too long.

I open the studio door to let it vent some fresh air into Becca's small art room.

My canvas of Jett's photo looks amazing; like some kind of shabby chic artwork you'd find in a high end shop.

I lightly touch the corner of the canvas, checking to see if the clear coat is dry yet. It feels like it, so I stand back and admire my work again. I'm not sure how I'll wrap it; covered in wrapping paper, or just presented with a pretty ribbon bow on the corner.

"Wow," Becca says, suddenly appearing in the doorway. I hadn't even heard her walk up the creaky stairs, probably because of the wind outside. "That looks amazing."

I've been keeping this project a secret from everyone, including my mom.

"Are you sure?" I ask, watching carefully for any signs that she's just saying that to be nice.

"Absolutely. I love what you did with this—was it transfer paper?"

I nod. "It's Jett's birthday present . . . Do you think he'll like it?"

She steps forward and lightly touches the side of the canvas. "Oh yes. He'll love it. This picture shows his dedication and hard work."

My chest tightens. Now that the project is over, I officially have his birthday present. Now I just hope he likes it as much as I do.

While Becca points out all the things she likes about the canvas, my brain starts stressing over what to get him for Christmas.

"What's wrong, honey?" Becca asks, her brows pulling in at the center.

I toss up my hands. "I still need a Christmas present for him. I can't think of anything to get."

"Hmm," she says, putting a finger to her lips.

"I need something extra nice. Something worth it." My feet begin to pace the small room.

"It's not the monetary value of the gift, Keanna. It's about the meaning of the gift. Think of something that will be special to him—even if it's cheap."

I heave a heavy sigh. "I'm not even concerned with the cost of it. I have money. What I don't have is ideas."

Becca follows me down to the living room, giving me advice but no real answers for gift ideas. "Try to think of something special to your relationship. Maybe an inside joke or a special memory?"

Her phone starts ringing from the kitchen so she squeezes my shoulder before leaving. "You'll figure it out."

Right. Sure, I will.

There's only a few days until Christmas and if I want to get him a gift, I'll need to do it soon. My phone buzzes just as I'm about to call Maya.

Jett: Shopping with D'andre is weird.

Me: lol. What are ya'll shopping for?

Jett: Can't tell you. It's a secret.

Me: Uh huh, sure. How much longer will you be?

Jett: At least an hour, maybe more.

Me: Cool, because I have some shopping to do with Maya.

Jett: I TOLD YOU I DON'T WANT ANYTHING

Me: Who says I'm shopping for you? :p

*

I'm so glad Maya agreed to go shopping with me. Since she already knew that our boyfriends were at the mall, she suggests going to an outdoor mall a little further away, that way we won't run into them.

I haven't been to this place yet and it's pretty awesome. There's a ton of clothing stores that I'd love to spend hours pursuing, but we have a goal. Christmas presents for the boys.

Maya holds up a men's sweater, frowning and then putting it back. "So, I have to admit I kind of freaked when I saw the Facebook drama about Jett being single again."

I snort. "Why?"

"Because I was like, no way. No way would they break up and she not tell me!" Maya laughs. "Then I felt like an idiot for believing it, of only for a short while. Ya know? God, I hate the media."

I run my hand across a rack of men's clothing. None of this would be a good match for Jett, but it is kind of the style D'andre likes so I'm stuck here for the time being. "I'm so over this media and fame crap."

"D'andre said you've been handling it like a pro.

Apparently you didn't even get mad when that breakup rumor hit."

I lift an eyebrow. "How did he know about t that?"

"Jett told him."

"Hmm." I didn't realize Jett talked about that kind of thing to his friends. Was I supposed to get pissed? Go on some kind of online rampage? It's not like that would have helped anything. People online are going to say whatever the hell they want, and if it pisses you off, then they'll only be happier.

"Okay, you look upset," she says as we leave one store and walk into another. "What's bothering you?"

I shrug and try to focus on all of the things in this store. "I'm not really so easy going about all of this crap. I actually *hate* Jett's popularity."

Her eyes widen. "You hide it well, girl."

"I know. I have to. I'm not about to be the girl who whines and complains every time I get jealous. That would only drive him away."

"True, but damn." Maya shakes her head. "I don't know if I could do it. I like D'andre because he's safe. He thinks I'm the best girl he could ever get so I feel secure, ya know?"

I laugh. "Probably don't tell him that."

She gives me an evil grin. "Don't worry, I won't."

"When it comes to security, I'm okay I guess. I mean, I know he loves me and I love him. But it's still not cool seeing all these girls swooning over him." My lip curls in disgust. "They touch him every chance they get. Little arm pats, or hand touching. Ugh. It takes everything I have not to go all Hulk Smash on those bitches."

She grids her fish into her hand. "If you need backup, let me know."

We laugh and leave another clothing store. The food court is up ahead, an all outdoors kiosk style place. At the corner is a massive store that's probably the biggest place in this whole shopping center. I've never heard of it before, but it says it's an *outdoors paradise.*

"What's this place?" I say, stopping to gaze into the massive windows. There's all kinds of fake rocks and waterfalls and trees decorating the shop. I see a pair of skis and tents and fake dogs in the window display.

"Some kind of outdoor place," Maya says. "My dad shops here a lot for his fishing gear."

My lips slide to the side of my mouth. It's an interesting place, for sure. Maybe there will be something in there to spark an idea for Jett's present. I turn to Maya. "Can we go in?"

"Girl you know I'm too feminine to care about anything

in that place." She glances down at her four inch heels and then grins. "But I'll suffer through it for you because I'm an awesome friend."

I reach for the door handle, which is a reclaimed tree branch and pull it open. "Good, because my women's intuition is telling me this might be the perfect place to find my dream gift."

Chapter 22

Jett

Keanna gives me this look that apologizes for what Becca is about to do. All I know is that I've just walked into their house and Becca yelled from somewhere out of sight that we have to wait in the kitchen until further notice.

I wrap my arms around Keanna and kiss her hello. "How was your day?"

"Very productive," she says, squeezing me tight. When she pulls away, her eyes flit to the oven. "I have officially gotten you the best Christmas present ever."

"Wrong," I say, shaking my head. "I got you the best present ever, so I guess yours is second best, but not *the* best."

She shakes her head and even her expression is stone cold confident. "You're wrong. I'm right. Get over it."

The oven timer dings and she rushes over, grabbing two oven mitts off the counter and taking out a glass dish that smells like Mexican heaven.

"What's this?" I say, walking over.

"Enchiladas." She sets down the dish and reaches for some plates. "You hungry?"

"Hell yeah," I say, taking out some forks from the silverware drawer. "This smells amazing."

She puts her hands on her hips. "Okay, confession time, Jett. If you're going to be with me for the foreseeable future—"

"Try forever," I say, holding up a finger.

"For *forever*," she says, grabbing a spatula and cutting the enchiladas apart. "So here's the confession—I'm not a good cook but I'm an okay preparer."

"What's the difference?"

She shrugs. "I made these with store bought tortillas, pre-shredded cheese, and canned sauce. I know a perfect girlfriend would have like secret family recipes and stuff, but I don't have anything except the recipes on the back of the box."

I take her hand and pull her across the tiled floor until our toes touch. I tilt her chin up to peer into her eyes. "You worry way too much my dear. You could make a bowl of cereal and I'd be forever grateful."

She makes this sad smile and then turns to grab a bag of tortilla chips from the pantry. "Becca makes all kinds of dinners from scratch. I don't know how she does it."

"She's also like twice your age babe. We have time to learn all that stuff. You don't need to stress about it now."

"Yeah, I guess you're right," she says, looking at the dish of enchiladas. "I guess because I'm out of school already, I feel like I need to be more grown up all the time."

"These are supposed to be the best years of our lives," I say. "We can be adults later."

Becca rushes into the kitchen, her face flushed. "Okay, I'm ready! Come on in," she says, waving for us to follow just before she disappears into the hallway. Keanna and I exchange a glance and then we find her in the new nursery room.

"What do you think?" Becca says, twirling around with her arms open. She's wearing a long black skirt and it flows with her, swooshing around her ankles when she stops.

I gaze around the room. It used to be a junk room but lately she's been transforming it into a nursery. The walls are pale green with little woodlands creatures painted along the walls. There's a crib and dresser and an old rocking horse given to her by her dad. But the grand masterpiece of the room is the tree.

Becca had a vision for it and hired someone to help her see it through. I remember hearing Keanna mention it offhand, but damn, this is amazing. The entire corner of the room is now a fake tree. The kind with a huge old trunk, hallowed out at the bottom to make a secret playroom. The fake branches extend up to the ceiling and run along for several feet, fake tree leaves dropping down.

"Your baby is going to have such a great childhood," I say, walking over to the tree's opening and peering inside. There's a little light hanging from the ceiling in here and pillows and a bookshelf filled with baby books.

"I'm so excited," Keanna says, gushing over all of the pieces of the room. "We still have so much to do but this is great!"

"I know, right?" Becca says.

"Wait, you have *more* to do?" I ask. "What more could you possibly do?"

They both look at each other like I'm just a clueless bum. "Oh honey," Keanna says, shaking her head. "You're so sweet and innocent."

"Babies come with a lot of stuff," Becca says. "I mean, look at our closet. There's not even any clothes yet!"

"You guys are weird," I say, just as the alarm on my phone goes off. I check it and my face falls. "Oh, shit. I can't believe I forgot."

Keanna looks confused for a split second and then recognition dawns on her face. "Your Skype interview."

"Yeah. Shit."

In just fifteen minutes, I'm supposed to be having a Skype interview with some motocross magazine online. They arranged it a few weeks ago, but I totally forgot. Apparently I'll be talking to the host and they'll ask me questions from fans. It's part of their social media marketing stuff.

"You could do it here," Keanna says. "Just use my computer."

"You don't mind?"

"Of course not. Just don't put me in the video and I'll be fine."

We agree to use her computer and have it facing a blank wall in her room so that my background will look nice and professional. While she sets it up, I scarf down three of her enchiladas and they're amazing, but I know if I tell her that'll just roll her eyes and say they could have been better.

While I wait for the magazine's social outreach coordinator—Brie Mason, according to my email—to call me on Skype, I try to remember our first phone call weeks ago. I've done plenty of interviews over the last couple of months and it's hard to remember what belongs to what.

Keanna's eyes go wide when Bree's Skype call starts ringing. She kisses me on the side of my head and gives me a quick hug. "Good luck!" she whispers just before I answer the call.

Bree is a hipster woman in her late thirties, her hair buzzed on the sides and dyed bright green on top. She wears thick black frames and has an interesting and badass looking tattoo on her neck. She explains to me that they're using a software that allows fans to call in and ask questions. Their video chat will be at the bottom of the screen, while hers will be up top. I'll be the main event though, my face nice and huge on the live stream and the video they'll keep on the site later on.

"Any questions before we begin?" she asks.

"Yeah," I say, feeling like an asshole. "What magazine was this for again?"

She laughs. "*Motocross Girls*"

"Oh, right." I give her what I hope is a charming smile. "That's what I thought."

Inwardly, I cringe. *Motocross Girls*? Does this mean what I think it means?

Yes, yes it does.

Bree's head is about two inches tall on Keanna's computer monitor. "Okay guys, our first question comes from MxGurl14."

Another little square pops up at the bottom of the screen and a young girl appears. Her cheeks are flushed, probably from nerves, and when she talks, her voice is all shaky.

"My questions is: Jett, do you think a girl could ever be a fast racer?"

"Absolutely," I say. "Girls can be just as badass on a dirt bike as a guy can be. I always tell people the key to being fast is to start as young as possible and work your butt off."

She grins and her pixelated cheeks turn red. "Cool. Thanks."

Bree introduces the next caller and this time it's an older girl, probably around my age. "Hi Jett," she says, waving flirtatiously at the screen. "I want to know, what do you look for in a girlfriend?"

"Uh, well," I say, looking toward Keanna's bed where she's no longer sitting since she left the room a few minutes ago. "I'm not currently looking for a girlfriend but when I was, I wanted someone sweet and kind. Someone I can trust."

"You could trust me, Jett," she says, tilting her head.

I don't know what it is about girls and that weird head tilt. I guess they think it makes them look sexy, or possibly like an innocent baby deer or something. Instead, it just makes it look like they're trying too hard.

The next few questions are all basically the same thing. Why did I agree to this interview, again? Was I temporarily insane? Probably.

Right after my internship went through, I got a little too excited about all the hype and attention I got. I would have agreed to anything.

Bree comes back on after about twelve callers. "Okay, it's time for some questions from our staff here at *Motocross Girls*."

Oh thank God, I think.

Bree asks me some questions that are legit motocross inquiries, and I'm happy to answer them.

Keanna stays away, probably to give me the privacy to work on this without distractions, but I miss her a lot. I'm also wondering if there's any more enchiladas left, but I'm betting Park has cleared out the leftovers by now.

"One final thing," Bree says. She adjusts her glasses and then grins. "A little birdie told us that your seventeenth birthday is tomorrow. Is that right?"

I chuckle. "Yep. That's right. I'm the Christmas Eve baby."

"Well, we have a special call for you next." She looks down at her keyboard and then a long window appears at the bottom of the screen. It's a video feed of about three dozen teenage girls. "Some of your biggest racing fans are here to sing you happy birthday."

They all sing the Happy Birthday song. Keanna walks

back in just when they're finishing and she breaks into a smile.

"Awesome," I say, clapping. "That was really cool. Thank you."

"*Thank you* for being here with us tonight!" Bree says. She says a few more things and then the call is officially over.

I look over at Keanna. "Well, that was fun and annoying."

She checks the time on her phone. "We still have four hours until midnight, when I want to give you your birthday present. Can you think of anything fun to do?"

"Actually," I say, swiveling in her desk chair until I'm facing her. "I have a great idea."

*

I decide to take Keanna to Shady Creek Heights, an uppity rich person subdivision two towns over. It's kind of a long drive, but I know it'll be worth it. It's Christmas Eve Eve after all, and everyone's lights will be on. Just before we arrive at the famed subdivision, I pull into a Starbucks and we get massive hot chocolates.

"So are you going to tell me where we're going yet?" Keanna says, blowing into the little hole on top of her hot chocolate lid. "I can't think of any place that's actually open this late besides Walmart."

"We're actually staying in the truck the whole time," I say cryptically.

Her lips move to the side of her mouth and then her eyes light up. "We're driving around to see something?"

I nod. She glances out the window and then gives me a knowing look. "Christmas lights."

"Yep." I steer the truck back onto the main road and take the exit for Shady Creek Heights.

This place has been on TV shows for its incredible Christmas lights display. The subdivision has about thirty mansions, all of which are owned by the super rich: athletes, doctors, and a few lesser famous celebrities and country singers. Every year, the neighborhood chooses a theme and all of the houses decorate according to it. I remember watching on one of those TV shows that participating in the holiday decorating is actually a rule in their homeowner's association. So this place is a big attraction and I'm excited to show her. I haven't been here since I was a kid.

"Oh my God," she says, putting her hand to her window.

We're only at the entrance of the neighborhood, but it's already spectacular. The brick entrance that spans on both sides of the gated entryway has been covered in a solid sheet of multicolored lights. A sign has been placed near the road.

Transiberian Orchestra Christmas! Tune in to channel FM 93.1 to listen!

I turn the radio to the right station and it begins playing one of the Transiberian Orchestra's amazing songs.

The guard at the gated entrance waves us through, saying visitors are allowed thirty minutes to drive through and check out the lights.

The tree-lined road is coved in lights that blink to the music. It is absolutely incredible. I barely remember to breathe as we take in house after house, each of them a beautiful mansion in their own right, but now they've been blanketed in LED lights that move to the music.

Waves of blue lights create a frozen lake that blinking penguins skate across. A holograph Santa walks across the roof of a house, then jumps into the chimney, disappearing in a starburst of lights.

Keanna's jaw drops and so does mine. We become completely overtaken by the beauty and the masterpiece of this neighborhood's Christmas display. Each house's design flows into the next one, creating Santa Claus' workshop, a gingerbread house, a candy cane lane, and a Christmas feast. The last house on the block has turned its roof and lawn into a three dimensional nativity scene, while still staying timed to the music.

It is absolutely breathtaking.

Half an hour later, we've idled through the whole neighborhood, and we make our way toward the exit. Dozens of cars are in front of and behind us, but I hadn't really noticed them until now.

"Wow." Keanna lets out a breath. "I feel like my life will never be the same again, now that I've seen that."

I grab her hand and then take a sip of my hot chocolate. "That was a thousand times cooler than when I came here as a kid, and back then it was still awesome."

"I'm glad you took me," she says. She unbuckles her seatbelt and slides over to the middle seat, leaning her head against my shoulder while we drive.

Once we're back in Lawson, I turn down a back road and we cruise around some more, looking at the random house lights we pass on the way.

"So, we have thirty minutes until midnight," she says, checking her phone for the time.

"What's so fancy about midnight?" I ask.

"It's your birthday, duh!"

I chuckle. "I think you care more about my birthday than I do."

"Well, I'm supposed to. I'm your girlfriend." She sticks out her tongue and I lean over to kiss her, almost missing a stop sign in the process. Luckily, we're in the middle of nowhere so there's no other cars around. "You look really hot tonight," I whisper into her ear before driving forward. "You always look hot," she says, giving me that seductive grin I love so much.

"There's a park up ahead," I say. "We should pull over and make out in the backseat."

She gives me this look. "That's something dumb teenagers do. We have bedrooms to use for making out."

I turn into the park anyway and choose a parking spot at the back. The lights are off and no one is here because it's so late at night. "Well, we are teenagers so . . ."

She leans over and slides her fingers into my hair. Her lips brush against mine. "So get in the back seat."

Chapter 23

KEANNA

I pull my clothes back on in the surprisingly roomy backseat of Jett's truck. My heart is pounding from another encounter with Jett and all of his special ways of making sure I feel loved. Jett sits up in the back seat, pulls his shirt over his head and then grins at me. His jeans are still unzipped, but at least they're on now. This whole time I'd been a little afraid that a cop would show up or worse—someone with a video camera. But we didn't take long, and no one so much as drove by. I guess Christmas Eve Eve isn't that big of a late night travel day.

My phone alarm goes off, alerting me that it's now midnight. I slide across the bench seat and crawl into Jett's lap. My head barely misses the roof of the truck, but I duck down to kiss him.

"Happy birthday."

"Thanks," he says, his fingers trailing down my chin. "I love you."

"I love you," I say between kissing him. "We need to get

to my house. I have a present for you."

"It can't wait until tomorrow?" he asks.

"It already *is* tomorrow," I point out. "Besides, I'm dying to give it to you."

"As you wish," Jett says. He opens the truck door and a cold burst of winter air fills the truck's cab. We get back in the front seat and as soon as we pull into his driveway, I realize the flaw in my plan.

His present is still on the third floor studio at home. Those stairs are creaky.

But I absolutely have to give him his gift at midnight. It's how I've been planning this whole thing. That way he'll get it now, then go back to sleep, wake up in the morning on his actual birthday and he'll have to wait a whole extra day to get his Christmas presents. It'll give the allusion that he's not getting gifts back to back, although he really is.

I don't know. Maybe it's lame. But maybe I'm just a lame person who enjoys these kind of things.

We sneak over to my house and I open the back door as quietly as possible. Although the Christmas tree's lights are still on, leaving a whimsical glow all throughout the living room, my parents are asleep.

I put my fingers to my lips and motion for Jett to follow me to the stairs. Going up to the second floor is easy because these stairs don't creak, but once you go down the hallway and face the much thinner row of stairs that lead to the studio, it gets a little shady.

"Be very quiet," I whisper, pressing my finger to his lips.

He pulls me into the darkened alcove at the base of the stairs and kisses me deeply, holding me tightly against his chest.

I kiss him back, getting lost in his touch until my head goes all lightheaded and swirly. I gasp for breath and step backward. "How dare you," I whisper, putting my hands on my hips.

"Sorry," he says, leaning in and kissing the crook of my neck. "I couldn't help myself."

I swallow, and try to gain control of my mind once again.

I step up on the first stair and then the second. If the wood creaks, I quickly shuffle to the other side. We walk slowly, Jett grabbing my ass on more than one occasion because it's right in his face, and eventually we get to the top of the stairs.

"I hope you like it," I whisper, my hand on the door. Only now am I getting really nervous. Making this project had been fun and even exciting, but now that I'm about to give it to him, I'm suddenly wondering if maybe it's not as great as I think.

I let out a nervous breath and open the door. Once we're inside, I close it behind us and then turn on the light.

I'd chosen to leave the canvas open, with only a silver bow on top. But I used some scrapbook paper and designed a big gift tag that hangs from the bottom. It says: HAPPY BIRTHDAY JETT, LOVE KEANNA in lettering that's big enough to read across the room.

"Whoa." Jett just stands here, his hand over his mouth.

I bite my lip so hard it starts to sting. "I made it," I say meekly, walking toward the canvas. I touch the side of it and watch him, judging for his reaction. "Do you like it?"

His shocked expression twists into one of excitement. "This is incredible. You *made* it? How?"

He walks forward and runs his hand down the shiny canvas. "Where did you get this picture?"

"I took it on my phone," I say, lifting my shoulders. This picture was taken in his quiet moment of personal reflection. He hadn't known I'd captured it to last forever. "I thought it was a special picture so . . ." I motion toward the canvas.

"This is the greatest thing ever," he says, not taking his eyes off it. "This is so much better than those professional shots of me racing or flying over a jump. This one is like . . ." he shakes his head and looks over at me. "This one is special.

Personal."

I grin. "Happy birthday, babe."

He wraps his arms around me and holds me tight. "Thank you."

*

I wake up the next morning to the sound of Christmas carols being played through the house's surround sound. I glance over at my phone and see that it's only eight in the morning. Ahhh . . .

But as tired as I am and as badly as I want to sleep in, I shuffle out of bed, yawn fifty thousand times, and head out into the kitchen. My new mom is grinning from ear to ear while she pours waffle mix into the waffle iron.

"Merry Christmas," she sing-songs as I pad into the room, rubbing sleep from my eyes.

"Merry Christmas," I say. I drop into one of the barstools on the other side of the kitchen island.

Park walks in from the back door, a bottle of syrup in his hand. "Morning, kiddo," he says, giving me a quick hug while he sets the syrup on the island. His jacket is freezing cold and it makes me shiver.

"Becca wanted waffles and we were out of syrup. It's a

good thing some stores are actually open on Christmas day." Park grins and reaches into his jacket pocket. "Merry Christmas, by the way."

He pulls out two scratch off lottery tickets and hands one to me and Becca.

"Cool," I say, taking the massive thing. It's as big as my head and boasts that you can win up to twenty times. "Thank you."

"He gets me one for every holiday," Becca explains. "That was sweet of you to get one for Keanna," she tells him.

Park winks at me and flips on the coffee pot. "She's my girl now, too."

Warmth fills me and it's not just from the hot air coming off the waffle iron. We scratch the lottery tickets and Becca wins twenty dollars and I win thirty-five. Not bad.

After breakfast, we head into the den, where the presents seem to have multiplied since the last time I was in here.

Although some of the gifts are for Becca's parents and relatives and Jace and Bayleigh, and some are the gifts Park and I got for Becca, most of them are for us.

Park and I open gift after gift, all of which make Becca smile and tear up when she sees our reactions.

"Mom, you should *not* have gotten me so many things," I say, looking up from a small box that contained a dozen gift cards to all my favorite fast food places. "This was way too much."

"Never!" she says, laughing. "I told you, I'm making up for eighteen years of gifts here." She looks around, reaches for another package that's wrapped in silver paper and shoves it in my hand. "So you're gonna open them and like them, missy."

"Yes ma'am," I say, tearing into the paper. It's a new wireless mouse for my laptop, which is perfect since I recently dropped mine on the patio and it shattered. Becca truly thinks of everything.

My new parents love the gifts I got them: home décor for Becca from her favorite boutique downtown, and new subscriptions to three of Park's favorite motocross magazines.

Becca sets up her camera on a tripod and gets a million family photos of our first Christmas together. Overall, it's the most amazing Christmas morning I've ever hand, and that's not because of the gifts involved. It's because for once in my life, I'm spending it with family, laughing and joking, and enjoying the morning. Christmases with Dawn were usually spent with her at work, or sleeping late, or telling me that Santa must not have been impressed with my behavior that year.

Bayleigh calls shortly after and insists that we come over as soon as possible. She's making a full Christmas meal for lunch but wants us over before that to hang out.

First, we open presents and although it's a little awkward at first, I feel more at home with Jett by my side.

His parents give me a charm bracelet from a very famous Texas jeweler named James Avery. The silver chain has heart-shaped links and they've added the dirt bike charm, a K+J charm, and one that says family. I tear up the moment I hold it in my hands. It is beautiful and thoughtful and I know I'll wear it forever.

Jett gets me a bunch of fun gifts that he knows I'll like, like a new case for my phone, and a gift card to the bookstore. I also get DVDs of my favorite shows that aren't on Netflix, and an entire stocking filled with my favorite kind of candy. My name is written on the top of the stocking in glitter and he admits he had to get his mom's help to make it look that pretty.

"Have you given her the . . ?" Bayleigh asks him after a while.

He shakes his head. "Not yet."

"Given me what?" I ask, peering at him. "You've already given me way too many things."

"Well, I have one more that's even more special."

"I have one more that's even more special for *you*," I say, poking him in the chest.

"Let's play rock paper scissors to see who goes first," he says, positioning his fist on top of his hand.

I play him and my rock beats his scissors. I squee and reach for the big box that I'd had to get Park to carry over here. It's not that it's too big, but it's way too heavy.

Everyone watches while Jett opens the box, revealing a massive camping backpack, filled with gear. But on the outside, safety pinned to the zipper so he sees it first, is his real present.

A week long hiking trip across the Guadalupe Mountains National Park, all-inclusive with a tour guide of our very own.

"You're coming too, right?" he asks.

I grin. "My backpack is at home."

He throws his arms around me. "This is amazing."

"Tell him the reason behind it," Becca says. I explain to him that I thought a camping and hiking trip would be a great way to destress after all of these motocross races. We'd be in the wilderness, connecting with Mother Nature, and away from all of the fame and annoying parts of the internet.

"This makes my gift look terrible," Jett says, laughing. He

reaches under the tree and takes out a small box. "But here you are. Merry Christmas."

I'm keenly aware of our parents watching me intently, but I try to block it out and just focus on Jett. Inside the box is a velvet jewelry box, long and rectangular. I pull open the lid and gasp.

It's a pink gold heart necklace, the heart is made of diamonds and I know without asking that they are real. I remember telling him that pink gold was so pretty and he must have remembered.

Tears flood into my eyes as I thank him, and he fastens it around my neck for me. Becca and Bayleigh coo over how pretty it is, and Jace tells his son he did a good job.

When all of the presents have been opened, we enjoy a Christmas feast around the Adams' dining table, and I eat until I'm totally stuffed.

It occurs to me, that in only a few months, a holiday that used to be meaningless to me has now become my favorite part of the whole year. I can see why Becca is so excited to share it with her future son. I can only imagine how much more magical it would be to experience all of this love and family as a child. But the past is in the past, and from now on, I'm living for a better future.

Chapter 24

Jett

It had taken me a while to decide on the perfect place to hang my artwork from Keanna. My dad thought it'd look great at The Track, but I wanted to keep it for myself, where I could see it any time. Plus, Keanna said she could always make more motocross themed canvases to hang up at The Track. This one in particular is mine.

I finally decide on mounting it directly above my headboard in my bedroom.

With a hammer and two nails, I hang it up and then step back to admire my handiwork. It looks great. Like the new focal point of my bedroom. I know I'm going to have this for a long time, and one day when I'm old, I'll be able to look back on my glory days.

Today is New Year's Eve, and my parents are throwing a big party at The Track. This has been their tradition for about five years now, and I'm only recently considered old enough to attend and drink the beer. The first couple of years, my parents only invited adults and it got kind of wild and crazy. They spare no expense for this party, calling it a way to 'give back to their clients' at the end of the year to use some of it as a tax write-off, I guess.

But Keanna is excited to attend, and even more so now that Becca and my mom have declared this party to be a masquerade. (I think they've been watching too many fancy shows on Netflix.)

The party theme is open to interpretation any way you'd like to, whether by dressing in a classic Victorian masquerade fashion with the fancy dresses, or by just wearing a mask. Hell, any mask would do, even one of those cheese plastic vampire masks for Halloween.

You can guess which way my girlfriend wanted to interpret it. The fancy way.

She'd spent the last few days scouring the city with Maya in an attempt to find the perfect Victorian-style dress. She'd told me she was going for something black and gold, the classic New Year's Eve colors. I'm guessing she found something suitable because yesterday she delivered my own ensemble for me. A black tux with a gold tie that has some kind of black baroque print on it. It matches the pocket square and I have a very masculine, if not tacky, black and gold face mask.

I haven't seen what she's wearing. Apparently, like

getting married, showing your fancy dress off before the big party is a big no-no. I'm excited though, because Keanna is excited. I'm happy to participate in whatever makes her eyes light up, no matter how silly it might seem to me.

After I'm all dressed in what feels like too many layers of fancy clothing, I head out to my truck and drive over to her house. The Track's parking lot is starting to fill up with catering vans and my parent's closer friends who show up early to things like this. Becca and Park walk outside just as I arrive. Park is dressed like normal, but he's wearing a plastic mardi gras mask over his face. Becca is wearing a long red gown that looks like it was salvaged from a vintage shop. Her mask is covered with an array of red and black feathers that go up taller than her fancy hairstyle. "You look so handsome," she says as our paths cross.

I thank her and then go inside, looking for Keanna. Her door is closed, but I go to walk in anyway and I nearly crash into it. It's locked.

I tap on the door with my knuckles. "Keanna? I'm here."

There's silence for a moment and then she says, "Go away."

"What?" My heart hammers in my chest. Have I done something wrong?

Then, on the other side of the door, she says, "No. Don't

go."

I lean against the door frame. "You okay?"

"No."

"What!" My panicked reply must startle her because the door unlocks and opens just a crack.

"I'm physically okay." One of her eyes watches me through the crack in the door. I know I could overpower her and shove my way inside if I wanted, but I give her the privacy she desires. She sighs. "I'm just not feeling very great about this dress."

"You've been raving about your dress for three days," I say.

"That was before I overheard your mom saying there's going to be two hundred guests tonight."

"So? It's a fun party, not everyone will be dressed up."

"That's not it," she says, pulling open the door further.

She's wearing a black gown with golden sequins sewn all over it in an intricate pattern. It's all very pretty, in a regal way instead of like what girls wear to prom.

"You look amazing," I say, taking her hands.

She frowns. "How many other girls will be there looking even better?"

I lift an eyebrow. "Zero. Exactly zero."

"You don't know that."

"Of course I do," I say, tilting her head up so I can kiss her. "There are no prettier girls than the most gorgeous girl on the planet."

She rolls her eyes but she smiles a little, so that's good.

"Baby, what's bothering you?" I ask, walking her over to her bed.

She lifts one shoulder and stares at the carpet. "I don't know. I *was* excited, but then I started thinking about all of your adoring fans and wondering how many of them will be here tonight."

She lifts the fabric of her skirt a few inches and then drops it disdainfully. "And how many of them will be dressed in revealing slutty clothes that make me look like some kind of prude weirdo?"

I can't help but laugh. "Baby, you're over thinking this. First of all, you're absolutely beautiful," I say, pointing to my finger. "Secondly, slutty girls aren't my thing, and thirdly—" I take her hand and bring it to my lips, kissing it. "You're the only girl I care about. For now, and forever."

"For*ever*?" she says, pronouncing it like two separate words.

There's a gift in my pocket that I've been saving for midnight. But I can't deny it—I'm thinking of giving it to her now. I gaze into her dark eyes, taking in all of her fear and insecurities. I wish I could wrap them all up, set them on fire, and insure that she never feels any kind of pain again.

"Forever, Keanna." I kiss her cheek. "This is our first New Years together. Let's make it special."

Chapter 25

KeaNNa

The party has transformed The Track into something magical. All of the grassy area between the main building and the track has been covered with those big white tents you see at weddings. There are three tents in all, each the size of a house. They all connect to a wooden dancefloor in the middle.

Clear lights and confetti and ice sculptures adorn every square inch of the place. There's a live band playing music, a catered dinner, and best of all: everyone wears a mask.

Some people took the silly approach like Park did, by wearing football mascot masks, or Halloween scary faces, but must people are more elegant, staying true to a classic Masquerade. I love every second of it.

And the best part?

Since we're all in masks, I can't really be compared to the other girls. No one knows when Jett and I enter the main tent, hand in hand. We're just two faceless people in a crowd of hundreds of others.

I can't believe I was so worried. If the masks stay on all night, I'll have no comparisons to other girls. It'll just be me and Jett.

Jett looks handsome as hell in his black, form-fitting tux. His mask is the male version of mine, so we match perfectly. It's taking everything I have not to shove him in a corner and make out all night. That would just be rude to our guests, right?

We sit at a table with other anonymous people and enjoy a dinner of salmon, wild rice and delicious veggies. Then, we walk around and mingle, and Jett eats something off every tray of finger foods we pass.

I spot Becca standing hear Park, her gorgeous red dress like a spotlight on her. We walk over and she recognizes me too, since we both helped each other get dressed.

"Having fun?" she asks, taking another sip of her champagne.

"Lots." In fact, my cheeks hurt from how much I'm smiling. I can't help myself. It's like a beautiful fairy tale in here.

Jett pulls me onto the dance floor, and although I'm horribly self-conscious and shy, he leans in and whispers, "No one knows who you are."

His words are like a magic spell that brings out the

dancer in me. We twirl and glide and hold each other close, our bodies moving to the beat of the music.

My waist starts to vibrate and I realize it's my phone. I had slipped it into the hidden dress pocket before I left my house, just in case I wanted to take pictures of anything. Now that I remember it's here, I take it out and ignore the phone call. It's a random number I don't know, so it's probably a telemarketer.

"Smile!" I say, holding it out and snapping a photo of Jett and me. Though our faces are covered, you can still see in our eyes and smiles that we're having a blast.

My phone rings again, vibrating with some unknown number. It's not even the same area code as the numbers around here I hit ignore and shove it back in my pocket.

Jett spies a tray of pigs-in-a-blanket, his favorite finger food, and scurries off to get some.

My phone vibrates again, only this time it's a text message.

Honey, please pick up.

What the hell? My hands turn to ice as I stare at the anonymous text message. Who else would call me *Honey*? Could it be her?

My throat goes dry. The phone begins to ring again. I catch Jett's attention as he shoves a finger food in his mouth and I point to the phone and then the door, letting him know I'm going to step outside to take this call.

Then my feet carry me as quickly as they can, through the blur of dancing strangers and out into the cool night air. I slide my finger across the answer key, and with a shaky hand, I bring the phone to my ear.

"Hello?"

"Keanna! My dear, how are you?"

My chest aches, but not from nostalgia. "I'm perfect."

I take a deep breath. All of the things I wanted to say in those first few weeks after she left me, all of the anger and betrayal I felt—I'm now just an empty shell of emotion. I can't be bothered to care anymore, so I keep my mouth shut.

"How are you, Dawn?" I ask.

"I'm okay, okay. But, I could use some money, dear."

I laugh out loud, a loud bark of sarcasm. "I don't have any money."

"No, dear, not from you of course. I mean from the Park's. Can you put Becca on the phone? I just need a small loan, or a gift, really. Just a few thousand dollars."

"You don't deserve anything," I say through gritted teeth. "Certainly not a gift."

"Keanna Byrd! How dare you speak like that!"

"My name is Keanna Park," I say, my breath coming out in little puffs of white air. "Don't call me again. You won't be getting any money from us."

"That is no way to speak to your mother," she hisses.

I clench the phone tightly to my ear. "You're right. But you are not my mother."

The cold air helps calm the anger that's coursing through my veins. I turn my phone completely off and then shove it back in my dress pocket. I will *not* let her ruin my New Year's Eve.

How could she even have the balls to call up out of the blue and ask for money? Seriously? She abandoned me. She let another couple legally adopt me without so much as telling me a final goodbye or that she loved me. But I've only ever been a burden to Dawn Byrd. Something she didn't want but couldn't find a way to get rid of until I was practically an adult.

I draw in a deep breath and turn back toward the party tent. I close my eyes and picture balling up all of this drama with my biological mother and throwing it in a trash. Then I tell myself I'll walk back into the party and I won't be pissed off anymore. I'll be over it. Because Dawn is not worth even two seconds of my time.

The tent is even more packed with guests now, happy drunken, dressed up guests. The music plays a lovely song, that has me swaying to the beat as I meander through the partiers, looking for my boyfriend.

Finally, I spot him, standing next to a tall cocktail table near one of the tent's clear fake windows. He's drinking a beer and talking with two guys who have put exactly zero thought into their masks.

As I make my way toward him, I see a girl in a skintight black mini dress, wearing the same black and gold eye mask as mine. I guess that's not too surprising; I'd gotten it at Charming Charlie, a fun girly store nearby.

She saunters up behind Jett, then taps him on the shoulder. Instinct has me annoyed, but I tell myself she doesn't know who he is—she's probably just being nice.

Wait.

What?

The whole room seems to blur into nothing as I watch the scene unfold. The girl, wearing my mask, taps his shoulder and he turns around. Then she grabs his face and pulls him into a kiss. She flings her body against his, grinding against him while she assaults his mouth with hers.

A pained gasp escapes my throat but the music is too loud for my pain to be heard. My legs keep walking somehow, and now I'm standing right in front of them. Jett's face scrunches beneath his mask and he pulls away, his lips turned into a scowl. The girl tries to grab him again but he looks up, almost confused.

Our eyes meet and I lift my mask off my face. A single tear rolls down my cheek as Jett makes the connection. The girl throwing herself on him is not me.

He shoves her back by the shoulder. "What the fuck?" he says, though it's barely audible.

The girl reaches for his hand and he yanks it away, then moves around the table to where I'm standing, still in shock.

"Baby, I'm so sorry," he says, his arm sliding around my waist. "I thought she was you."

"I know." I nod because my voice is too choked up to understand. "I saw it."

The mask girl twirls around, then puts her hands on her hips. Her blue eyes bore into mine and her lips twist into a smirk. "You're not good enough for him, you know."

"Who the fuck are you?" Without realizing it, I'd thrown my body forward to launch at her, but Jett holds me back.

"Don't, baby. It's not worth it."

"You're trash," she tells me, her voice confident. "He'll never be good enough for you."

"Get out of here," Jett tells her. He points to the door like she's a bad dog who lost her indoor privileges. "Go and don't come back."

My chest heaves and my hands are shaky. Without another word, I turn on my heel and rush out of the tent. I need air. Cold air, fresh air. Air away from all of these people.

I bump into a few shoulders but I don't care. Soon, I burst free from the tent and I'm in the dark, running into the parking lot. I make it all the way through the rows of cars until I'm standing near the road. The music is just a soft thumping sound in the distance. I am finally alone.

I pitch forward, resting my hands on my knees. This gravel parking lot has probably ruined my black velvet heels, but I don't care.

Between Dawn calling me for the first time in months, and seeing some bitch take advantage of my boyfriend and then tell me I'm not good enough—the one fear I can't ever seem to shake—I can't handle this.

I need to be alone. I need a moment to breathe.

"What's wrong there, girly?" The slurred male voice startles me. It seems to have appeared out of thin air.

"Nothing, I'm fine," I call out, without turning around. I stand and wipe the tears from my eyes as I gaze out the county road in front of me, the vast endless horse pastures beyond. The moon overhead casts a glow on a small pond in the distance.

"Looks like somethin's wrong," the guy says. He sounds closer.

"I'm fine, really." I wave a hand through the air. "You can leave."

A sweaty hand wraps around my wrist, pulling it behind my back. I stiffen, my entire body going into panic mode. Warm breath hits my ear. "You look like you could use some cheering up, darlin'."

My heart seizes in my throat. Another hand grabs my ass, squeezing it so hard I wince.

"Let me go," I say, my voice trembling. I need to run. But my feet won't move. I am stuck, dammit. I am frozen. *Move.*

I'm spun around against my will and a guy in his twenties, wearing ratty clothing and no mask at all gives me a look that chills me to the core. His grin is pure evil.

"What do we have here?" he says, his eyes roaming down my body. With a death grip on my wrist, his other hand grabs my boob.

"Get off me!" I yell, happy to have found my voice. I strain to move but he holds me against him, the air smelling like stale cigarettes and body odor.

He grabs my dress and pulls it up until my whole hip is exposed. I wriggle and struggle to get away but he's too strong. "You're a hot mess," he says, running his hand up my thigh.

Tears burn my eyes and I pull so hard it feels like my wrist is going to break. Good, I don't care. I just want away from this creep.

His rough hand inches up my thigh and I scream. I scream as loud as I can. His grip lessens and then he's throw backward.

Jett's mask flies to the ground and he plummets his fist into the guy's face, then kicks him right in the stomach, making him fall to the gravel.

"Call the police," Jett tells me, meeting my eyes for just a second before he unleashes on the guy, pounding his face into the ground. He flips him to his stomach and pulls his arms around his back. Jett's knee digs into his shoulder blades and he uses the guy's own arm to choke him.

I take out my phone and wait for it to power up, which seems to take forever. My fingers are shaky but I get the numbers pressed. I tell them I was attacked by a strange man.

Soon, police cars show up and the guy is arrested. It all happens so fast.

Jett talks to the officers and then they talk to me. It turns out the guy was home hobo and also a criminal. He wasn't invited to the party; he had just been passing by when he happened to see me walk to the road. He's assaulted women before. The police ask if I'd like to press charges.

Jett holds my hand and looks me in the eyes. "He shouldn't be allowed to hurt people and get away with it," he says.

I look to the officers. I tell them yes.

Chapter 26

Jett

It feels out of place being so full of *rip-someone's-face-off* anger while wearing a fancy suit. Once the police leave, I can tell Keanna is still shaken up. If I hadn't arrived when I did—well, I can't think about that. I might actually rip someone's face off.

I can't believe my girl got attacked because of some bitch who tried to trick me into making out with her. If that hadn't happened, she would have never run outside, prompting me to look everywhere for her. That homeless criminal would have never gotten his hands on her.

My fist aches to punch something.

"You okay, son?" Dad's brows are pulled together. He's been out here since the police arrived, helping Keanna and me get through the whole ordeal. We'd insisted that everyone else stay at the party, keeping up the fun so that the whole night wouldn't be ruined.

I squeeze my shoulders together then relax them. "I guess. I'm just pissed."

"That's normal," he says, lowering his gaze on mine. "But you need to be strong for Keanna, okay? She'll probably be freaked out for a while."

He has no idea. Now not only does she have to deal with being groped by some asshole, she's also hurt from watching another girl kiss me. But Dad doesn't know that part and I have no intentions of telling him.

I nod once and let out the breath I'd been holding. Staying so pissed off won't help anything. "I need to find Keanna," I say. Dad steps out of the way and I walk over to where Mom and Becca are talking with her.

When she sees me, her sad eyes look straight into mine and she walks into my arms.

"Sorry for all the drama," she mumbles into my chest.

"You have nothing to be sorry about," I say, kissing the top of her head.

Becca and Mom watch me like I'm some kind of puppy or something. I don't think they'll ever treat me like an adult after seeing me as their kid for so long.

"Honey, ya'll take some time alone and if you feel like getting back to the party, we'll be here, okay?" Mom smiles and hands me my face mask. I don't know where I dropped it earlier, I only remember throwing it out of the way. Our two moms leave and then I'm left alone with my girl, near the entrance to the main tent.

"Can we just not talk about this anymore?" Keanna says, gazing up at me. Her eye makeup is all streaked from crying, but she lowers her mask back over her face, and now it doesn't matter. "I want to at least *try* to have some fun tonight."

My hands slide down her arms, my fingers weaving with her fingers. "Of course. It's almost midnight."

"Good," she says, rolling her eyes. "I am ready for this year to be over."

I chuckle. I want to kiss her so bad, but I'm not sure if that's the right move after she was just traumatized. The little box in my jacket pocket is burning a hole in me. This was supposed to be a magical party full of love and romance, where I gave her this gift under a moonlit night of perfection. Instead, it's all kind of gone to hell.

But maybe I can still salvage the night.

"Will you walk with me?" I ask, holding out my elbow like they did in the old fashioned movies.

She links her arm in mine. "I don't see the harm in walking when I have you with me."

I grin. "Nothing will ever happen to you when you're with me."

Her head rests against my arm as we walk through the

party, then head outside near the bleachers. I consider bringing her out to the back of the track where we had that picnic one time, but it's too dark and we're not wearing the right clothes for a dirt bike ride. I think the bleachers will have to do.

I glance behind us to insure that we're alone. The party rages on behind us, everyone keeping inside the tents because that's where the portable heaters and booze are.

"So," I say, swallowing. There was a whole speech I'd had planned out, an entire thing. I've been reciting it in the shower for a week and yet now, it's all gone. Not a single word remains in my memory. I look over at her, hoping to glean some inspiration from her beautiful face.

Only, she's crying.

I stop just short of the first row of bleachers. "Baby, why are you crying? Is it because of that asshole, because he's going to be locked up for a long time. Plus, we've got a restraining order—"

"No. It's not that. It's not him." She lifts her eye mask off her face and sets it on the bleachers, then she dries her eyes with the back of her hand.

"Can we sit?" she asks, gazing up at me with those innocent but pained eyes.

I sit on the bottom bleacher and she joins me, leaning

toward me so that our knees touch. My heart thumps like a freaking jackhammer. I have no idea what she's going to say but it's terrifying.

She frowns and looks at her lap. "Earlier, before that girl—"

"Honey, I swear I had no idea she wasn't you at first. It was like two seconds and then I realized it. I shoved her away."

She shakes her head. "No, I know. I saw it all. That's not what I'm talking about."

Okay, now I'm even more freaked out. "Go on," I say. "Whatever's on your mind, I want to know."

She swallows and looks up at me. "Dawn called me today."

My jaw tightens. Of all the days to call the daughter you threw away, she had to pick this day? The last day of the year that I had planned to make special for my girlfriend.

"I know," Keanna says, after seeing my reaction. "And you know the worst part? She just wanted money. No apology, no asking how I'm doing. Just asking for money."

I take in a breath through my nose and let it out in a huff. "You are too good to be born to someone like that."

"I agree with you on that one," she says, making this sad little smile. "Even if I was really poor and alone and couldn't afford a kid. If I *had* one, I'd love it and take care of it. I know I would. I don't know how anyone could put their own happiness over a child's. It's not like I *asked* to be born."

"You are not like her in any way." I bend down and kiss her. To my surprise, she takes my head in her hands and deepens the kiss.

"Now that's more like it," she says, grinning as she pulls away. "Only my lips get to touch yours."

"You seem a little happier now." I take her hand and bring it up to my lips.

She nods. "I don't really want to waste all this time talking about Dawn. I basically told her to fuck off and then I blocked her number, so we're good. I just wanted to let you know that it happened but now I want to forget all about it. Does that make me weird?"

"Not at all," I say. There's a loud cheering coming from the party so I check the time on my phone. "Two minutes until midnight."

"What is it you wanted to say?" Keanna asks, nudging me with her elbow.

I lick my lips. "How'd you know I wanted to say something?"

She gives me a look. "You were stuttering and tripping over your words the whole way over here, Jett. I'm not stupid."

I sigh and look up at the sky, gazing at the bright moon above us. "You are too smart for me," I say, shaking my head. "But, you're right. There is something I needed to say."

I know I shouldn't get down on one knee—this isn't exactly that kind of thing. But sitting on the bleachers feels weird, too.

"Keanna," I begin, as I stand and take her hands to pull her up next to me. "I have a present for you. It's more of a promise, really."

Her eyes widen in curiosity. The moonlight makes her look like a damn angel and in this moment, my chest hurts so bad. I am so lucky to have this girl in my life, to have her be mine. She loves me, and I love her.

Words pour of out me, and they aren't exactly like I'd rehearsed but I think they get the job done.

"You are my soulmate, Keanna Park. I love you and I love everything about you. In less than a minute, we're going to start a new year together, and I want you to know that this is the start of everything for us. Not just one year, but every year, forever." I reach into my pocket and take out the small box. "I know we're too young for actual marriage, so I'm doing something else." I open the box, and Keanna gasps. Tears fill her eyes, but for once tonight, they are good tears.

"This is a promise to you," I say, taking out the pink gold ring. Its heart-shaped diamond sparkles like crazy beneath the stars, and Keanna lifts a shaky hand to me so I can place the ring on her finger. "It's a promise that you'll always be mine, forever and ever, and that one day," I say, gazing into her eyes, "one day I'll marry you."

From back at the party, everyone begins the countdown to the New Year. "Ten . . . nine . . . eight!"

Keanna watches me with a look of awe. She looks at the ring on her finger and then throws her arms around me. "Thank you," she whispers.

"Four! Three!"

She pulls back and we gaze into each other's eyes while the crowd at the party counts down to zero. A roar of cheers bursts out and I kiss her, long and passionately, bringing us into the New Year in the most perfect way possible.

Epilogue

Five months later

I burst into the waiting room, startling not only Jett but the random couple in the corner. "Sorry," I say, giving them an apologetic wave. Then I dive straight toward Jett, who'd been sleeping in the uncomfortable hospital chair.

"He's here!" I say, unable to contain my excitement. "He's here, he's here, he's here!"

Jett rises and wraps me into a massive bear hug. Becca had insisted that I be in the delivery room with her and Bayleigh. Park and Jace decided to stand just outside the door so that the room wouldn't be too crowded, and Jett had kindly offered to sit in the waiting room. I think the idea of a baby being born is kinda gross to him.

"His name is Elijah," I say as I take Jett by the hand and pull him toward Bayleigh's delivery room. "And he's perfect. Absolutely perfect."

"Someone sounds like they're already an impeccable big sister," he says, bumping into me.

I can't stop my grin because I am truly so excited for my new family. We enter the room at the same time Park and Jace are leaving, both of them wearing these proud fatherly grins. There is so much more than friendship between these two married couples. It's like we're all one big family.

I poke my head in the room and Becca motions for us to enter. She's standing, holding her new baby in her arms. Bayleigh is in the hospital bed, looking tired yet somehow still radiant. Jett walks over and hugs his mom and then comes to see the baby.

"You're right," he says, watching Elijah with sense of pride in his eyes. "This is one adorable baby."

"Thank you, dear," Becca says. She kisses her newborn on the forehead and then turns to me and smiles. "Last year I had no kids and now I have two."

The way she says it brings tears to my eyes. I lean against her and watch my baby brother, who is fast asleep. He hasn't even been on earth a whole hour yet, and here I am feeling more love than I'd ever known was possible. I know for a fact that I'll never let anything or anyone hurt this little guy.

Later, Park brings in an enormous amount of Chinese takeout and we all sit around Bayleigh's hospital room and eat it, family style.

"So was it easier or harder having a baby the second time?" Jett asks his mom.

She considers it for a moment, her egg roll dangling over the sweet and sour sauce. "You know, I think it was easier.

But only because I wanted to do a really good job for my best friend. I wasn't about to let this labor take forever," she says with a laugh. "I wanted Becca to get her son ASAP."

Becca laughs and Elijah yawns from his clear plastic nursery bed.

"Are you already tired, little man?" Jett asks him. He looks up at Park. "We need to get your kid in shape if we want to make him the next motocross superstar," he says with a smirk.

Park nods. "I made an appointment with his personal trainer for tomorrow morning."

Becca swats at her husband. "Oh hush.

"So," Bayleigh says, looking over at Jace. "We have a little announcement for you all."

Jace hurries to finish his bite of food and then gets up and sits next to her on the hospital bed. "Are you telling them or should I?"

They stare at each other for a moment, lost in their own little world. Finally, Bayleigh grins. "I'll do it." Then she turns to us, her smile stretching across her whole face. "We want to have another baby!"

Stunned silence fills the room and then Becca breaks into a cheer. "Oh my God! We'll have babies at the same time!"

"I know," Bayleigh says, a child-like excitement on her

face. "I figure our two older kids are all grown up now, so why not?"

"I am so excited," Becca says, clasping her hands in front of her chest.

"Keanna," Bayleigh says, looking at me. She points her fork between Jett and me. "You two need to figure out your wedding dates because I refuse to be pregnant and fat at the wedding, okay? We need to work around it."

My cheeks flush. I glance down at my promise ring, a gorgeous piece of jewelry that probably cost more than most people's engagement rings. "Um," I say, but Bayleigh waves a hand at me.

"Don't play cool, girlfriend. We all know you and my son are meant to be together. Hell, Becca and I have practically planned your whole wedding already."

I turn to the left and bury my face into Jett's shoulder. My cheeks are so red hot right now I'm afraid they'll get a third degree burn.

"Don't worry," Jett says, patting my back. "The first thing we'll do after we get married is move far *far* away from these lunatics."

"HA!" Bayleigh says. "Keanna's not going anywhere, son. She loves us. Isn't that right, Becca?"

"It's right," Becca says, giving me a wink. "You're stuck

with us forever, Jett."

"Yep," Bayleigh says. "Forever."

***

Thank you for reading Believe in Forever! If you enjoyed the book, please consider leaving a review on Amazon or Goodreads.

Want to get an email when Amy's next book is released? Sign up for her newsletter here:
http://eepurl.com/bTmkPX

Don't miss Amy's new release: Ella's Twisted Senior Year **Available on Amazon**.

A tornado destroyed her home, but can it repair her future?

Want more motocross? Check out the Motocross Me series, written by Amy's other pen name, Cheyanne Young. **Available on Amazon**.

About the Author

Amy Sparling is the author of The Summer Unplugged Series, The Devin and Tobey Series, Deadbeat & other awesome books for younger teens. She also writes books for older teens under the pen name Cheyanne Young. She lives in Houston, Texas with her family and a super spoiled rotten puppy.

Amy loves getting messages from her readers and responds to every single one! Connect with her on one of the links below.

Connect with Amy online!

Website: **www.AmySparling.com**
Twitter: **twitter.com/Amy_Sparling**
Instagram: **instagram.com/writeamysparling**

58318889R00132

Made in the USA
Lexington, KY
08 December 2016